AND THEN THERE WERE MORE

E.A. Petersen

ACKNOWLEDGMENTS

Many thanks to my editor and publisher, Izzy Findlay, for her help in pushing me to finish the third book of the Cliff Marks series. The medical crisis that has affected the world the last two years has almost crushed the creative spirit and joy of writing. We both kept going to get it done.

FROM THE AUTHOR

I am no student of the inner workings of the US Congress, so I probably bend the rules to fit the storyline. Hopefully, most readers will be like me and not know fact from fiction.

TABLE OF CONTENTS

CHAPTER 1: THE FIRE BOMBERS

She heard the crash of glass. A whiskey bottle full of gasoline struck the sill of the bedroom window before exploding into a fireball. The blaze lit up the room as Gloria bolted from the bed. She noticed that none of the flames had infiltrated their bedroom. As she was shaking Cliff awake, the second gasoline-filled bottle hit slightly left of the window, the ignited fuel now running benignly down the side of the building's brick walls.

Gloria heard voices shouting from the lawn below the window, and then several gunshots. A security guard knocked on the bedroom door and asked if they were alright. She could hear the unintelligible squawking from the security guard's portable radio. Gloria shouted back, "We're okay!" before slipping on her bathrobe.

Cliff, now fully awake from all the noise, was sitting on the edge of the bed when Gloria headed out the bedroom door. He could hear sirens in the distance as he walked out of the bathroom; he started getting dressed, even though it was 3:00 a.m. The household was gathered in the kitchen when Cliff shuffled in, hoping someone had made coffee. He tried shutting out all the excited kitchen chatter until he had his coffee. He could see Gloria jabbing a finger toward the chest of one of the security guards. Cliff knew she was furious that intruders had breached the compound – and that they had been close enough to hit the house with a hand-thrown, homemade liquid bomb.

Most everyone returned to their rooms as Cliff sipped his second cup of coffee. A member of the household staff ushered Kansas City Police Captain Greg Sands into the kitchen. Sands was aware this was a congressman's home, and that Marks had a special relationship with the chief. Sands heard rumors that Marks helped free him from the influence of a corrupt local politician, John Kingsley. Plus, he had an unusual contract with the police department as a consultant.

"No offense intended, Captain Sands, but talk to my wife. She deals with security," said Marks, holding up his left hand before the captain could speak.

"None taken, sir. I'm not here to deal with the firebombing. The detectives will handle that. I was instructed to make sure you were alright. You have a lot of friends in high places."

"Thank them for their concern. Join me for some coffee," said Marks, pulling out one of the tall chairs from the large kitchen island.

Sands deferred for a moment, but accepted the offer and sat down. It was not often that he got a one-on-one with a congressman.

"I heard your wife talking with your security guards as I came in the house. She was chewing on them pretty hard."

"My wife doesn't accept second best. There are plenty of security guards who would love to have this job. They get paid very well compared to their contemporaries in the security guard business."

"I heard you had security guards with you 24/7, even before you were elected. Because of tonight, I can see you need them, but I'm not sure why…" Sands trailed off.

Marks gave his usual explanation. "You can make a lot of enemies being in the detective business. The bad guys take exception to people messing with them. We write their cost off as a business expense. We use them from time to time to do some fact-finding and security for the agency. This isn't the first incident, and it won't be the last. Every time we've been attacked, the bad guys end up dead, seriously wounded, or in jail. As you can see, I'm not concerned. My wife will figure out our defense's weak spots and will fix them," Marks clarified, as he refilled his coffee mug then Sands's.

"I saw the video of your wife taking on the commissioner's security detail. Everyone was blown away. We give her a wide berth," said Sands, smiling.

"The scary thing is, she enjoys it and looks forward to the fight," replied Marks, right as Gloria strolled into the kitchen.

"Cliff, do you want to talk to them?" she asked.

"Sure, bring them in."

"No, you come outside. I don't want them in my house. They're in the back of the police cruisers," Gloria insisted.

"Yes, ma'am," said Marks, shrugging his shoulders and grinning at Sands. "I also give her a wide berth."

Marks continued, "Captain, would you speak with the arresting officers to see if I could have some privacy with these hooligans? Nothing physical, just talk," he added when he saw the look of concern on Captain Sands's face.

"Sure, Congressman Marks."

Marks waited a couple minutes before going outside. There was someone in the wire-caged backseat of both cruisers. Marks recognized Cloy Probst, the henchman that worked for the former mayor, and his political opponent in the election, Kingsley.

"Probst, I see you didn't take my advice to move on from your relationship with Kingsley."

There was a long silence before Probst spoke. "He told me he'd go after my family if I didn't continue working for him."

"Whose idea was this firebombing?"

"His. He wanted to scare the hell out of you."

"Not kill us?"

"Oh, he wants you dead. After the failed attempt to kill you before the election, he realized he needed more planning and better people. This firebombing was meant to keep you looking over your shoulder while he finds some real mercenaries. I wasn't going to firebomb the entrances to the house. I wanted everyone to get out."

"How thoughtful," said Marks, sarcastically. "Your plan didn't get very far."

"We didn't know you had so much security," replied Probst.

"Obviously not enough! You got so close to the house."

"Yeah, but we were only able to throw two bottles; we had a dozen. We were supposed to light up the house on all four sides. I think they thought we were going to break into the house because I was carrying a bag that could've been full of burglary tools. My guess is they were going to let us break into the house, so we could be charged with more than simple trespassing. It surprised the shit out of them when we pulled a couple bottles from the bag and lit the gas-soaked rags sticking out of them. I heard the guards yelling as they came rushing toward us. I'm sure they finally realized their idea to delay grabbing us was dumb...and dumber when the two bottles hit next to your bedroom window."

"Who's your sidekick?" Marks asked.

"Louie, a junkie I've known since childhood. He'll do anything to support his habit."

"Where's Kingsley?"

"Not sure. I did see a travel brochure for Peru on his desk. It's not over. He'll be back. I've never seen him so angry as when he lost the election. He was screaming and throwing things."

Marks heard all he needed to know and exited the cruiser. He went back in the house and told Gloria what he learned from Probst.

"Of course, he lied to me when I asked him where his boss was. Kingsley is in Quebec City, Canada...not Peru. I'm thinking about sending a couple of Club Car members on a vacation to pop in on Kingsley and give him our compliments."

"Nothing physical, right?" asked Gloria.

"No, no. They'll just mess with his mind – like sitting next to him at a café and talking about the firebombing of our house, parking next to him in a vintage car with the convertible top down, or how about sending a fruit basket to his hotel room with a card? *Looking forward to your return to Kansas City, signed Gloria and Cliff Marks'.*"

"No harassing phone calls or emails?"

"None. It's against the law."

"Stalking?" Gloria was insistent that they didn't do anything illegal.

"I'll have them talk with Buhrowe before they go, okay?"

"They'll need passports."

"Gloria," said Marks, giving her a look. "I've got this."

"Sorry, Cliff."

"What happened with the security detail?"

"Underestimated the enemy. You remember our sharpshooter, Alexis Perry, who saved our asses when we were rammed by the Hummer. She was going to turn the dogs loose and grab them as soon as they came over the wall. Her boss wanted to see what the intruders were going to do. Dumb! Now she's the captain of the security detail," said Gloria.

"What do you call that – a battlefield commission? Way to go, wife!" said Marks, giving her a high-five.

"I know you handle the security guards, but would you mind if I talked to your new captain?" asked Cliff.

"I don't mind. You want to speak with her now?"

"Yes."

"Okay, I'll go get her."

Alexis Perry stood six feet tall, with a physique that looked like she could take care of herself in any situation. She had thick red hair cut short, with Doris Day freckles and a pleasant face.

When Alexis came in the kitchen, she stood at attention. Marks did not tell her otherwise.

"My wife usually handles the security personnel, but now seemed like a good time for me to let you know what you'll be up against in the future. The incident, when your courage and skill saved our lives, was orchestrated by the same man who directed the firebombing tonight. He won't stop trying to kill me – ever. His name is Kingsley, and he's beyond angry that he lost the election to a Johnny-Come-Lately like me and that I've been involved in slowly exposing his corrupt organization in Kansas City. He's powerful, totally ruthless, and very wealthy. He's an adversary that cannot be ignored. I didn't want you to think that these attacks were random events. There will be more until one of us is dead," he paused before continuing.

"Maybe some of our security staff didn't sign up for a job that could be this lethal. The two men that you killed were local deer hunters who were desperate for money. They were amateurs. So were the two firebombers. I don't think Kingsley will go cheap in the future by hiring local, untested talent; instead, he'll look for professional mercenaries to do his killing. Gloria will contact your boss, Mr. Crawford, tomorrow, so he can brief the entire staff that their jobs are – and will become – more dangerous. That said, when Gloria and I are together, you go with us. You pick the backup teams when you need a break. If you need anything to improve your capability, we'll get it for you. Make a list and my wife will provide the money. Your concern is not the cost. Your only concern is the security and safety for yourself, my wife, and me. Any questions, Alexis?" Marks explained, matter-of-factly.

"Yes, sir…but it's off-subject."

"Ask away," said Marks.

"Stu Nichols is a friend of yours?"

"Yes."

"Do you object to me starting a relationship with him?"

"You have some competition," Marks replied, smiling.

"Yes, I've seen Margaret Koluccy's eyes light up when she's around Stu."

"Do his eyes light up?"

"Not hardly. I don't think he's comfortable around a Ferrari like Koluccy. He's more likely to go for a Ford F-150…like me," Alexis speculated.

"I have no objection. What about you, wife?" Marks asked Gloria.

"I'll enjoy the show," she replied.

"Tell you what – the next time Koluccy is in Washington, I'll make sure you and Stu are also there. It'll be interesting to see who can get him in bed first," said Marks.

"No, I want to see who the alpha dog wants to get in bed with. It's easy for a woman to get a man in bed...but with that approach, the possibility of longevity in the relationship is flimsy," Alexis explained.

"The wife has already cooked up a plot to get Stu married. She's going to encourage Koluccy to do some sunbathing poolside – in a bikini, of course – when Stu arrives on scene. You want to join in?"

"No, I'll be floating in the pool in an inner tube. I'll bet he jumps in with me to get away from the obvious honey trap. Will that be all, sir?"

"Yes. Good evening, Captain Perry."

"Goodnight then."

Alexis gave the military about-face and left the room.

CHAPTER 2: MY HOME TO YOUR HOUSE

The pending move to Washington DC caused a stir of excitement amongst Marks's staffers, particularly regarding who would be selected to move with him. They quickly began jockeying for position with their boss, Margaret Koluccy. She knew none of the campaign staff were going to Washington, and that Marks was only taking his longtime friend, Jerome Sparker. She avoided the staff's bombardment of questions, assuaging their concerns by telling them they would be on the payroll for the next six months, and everyone would be needed for the congressional office in Kansas City, since some staff members were leaving to pursue other jobs. Additionally, the staff were welcome to live in Marks's Kansas City mansion rent-free.

Gloria and Cliff thought Walter Champion was kidding when he showed them photos of the DC mansion, called 'Gleason,' then told them they could live there. All they had to bring was their clothes and personal things.

It took 10 large wardrobe boxes and six medium boxes to transport Gloria's clothes and shoes. Only two boxes, one large and one medium, for Marks. Their lawyer, Dick Buhrowe, stated that it was legal to use campaign funds to ship their personal belongings, so UPS picked up the boxes two days before their departure to DC.

The Markses spent a full day making the rounds to thank people for their friendship and support. It was a long list of individuals, starting with four doctors at St. Luke's Hospital, the Car Club members, his campaign staff, the coma patients he revived, Stu, Bonneville, Jordan, Jameson, Margaret, a tearful goodbye from Robby, dinner with Gloria's parents, the gang at the De Ville Detective Agency, US District Attorney Robert Speelman, Captain Curt Chesney, and ending with the Syntil executives.

"Cliff, I want you to know that Jordan Walker and Dr. Candle will take care of Robby like a son. They'll continue to monitor his rehab and the development of his implant's integration with his brain. On another note, I hope you'll invite us to come to Gleason. It's such an amazing place, and I know you'll enjoy living there. By the way, you can use its allure to your political advantage," hinted Champion.

"Never forget that our operations center always has your back and sees what you see 24/7. We all read their daily reports on your activities. We aren't here to micromanage your life. You have repeatedly demonstrated that you always act in Syntil's, and the country's, best interests. Our only concern is your and Gloria's safety, as well as the secrecy of the implant program," said Lance Winford.

"Gloria and I will never forget who made all of this possible. Many thanks."

Jerome was tasked with checking out Marks's congressional office. He assumed that since Scott Browning, whom Marks replaced in the House, was elected to the Senate, would recruit his former staffers to come work for him. One staff member, Becky Smoot, was left behind. Jerome asked her to educate him and the congressman about the de facto function of the House, sometimes outside the strict letter of the law. They had both read the rules about the House, yet knew that the de jure operation of how Congress was supposed to lawfully and officially conduct business, might not be the way things happened in reality.

Becky Smoot was, by any definition, a huge woman – all 5 feet 10 inches, 300 pounds of her. She had a beautifully flawless complexion, along with a sweet personality. Her hair, clothes, and makeup were perfect. Becky Smoot was the ideal person to meet and greet office visitors. She charmed everyone she met, including Jerome, Gail, and Margaret.

Marks was distressed about Ms. Smoot's weight; he wondered how he could broach the subject with her. He activated his implant to research numerous books and articles about diet and weight loss. Every doctor, nutritionist, personal fitness trainer, TV personality, and health guru that authored a book thought they had the perfect solution. In reality, none of the experts could control the dieter's thoughts, willpower, or desires;

however, Marks could because he knew what they were thinking and could plant ideas in their minds.

The second time Marks met with Ms. Smoot, he told her – telepathically, of course – that she hated anything sweet. Marks watched her face as he planted the thought in her mind. She cocked her head and lowered her chin slightly. Her eyes had a strange, quizzical look, as if she were in another world, one she did not recognize. Without a word, Ms. Smoot left the foyer, where she and Marks were standing, went to her desk (one of four in the outer office), and sat down. Marks let her be as her mind tried to figure out what had happened. She heard someone speaking to her, not through her ears, but from inside her head.

Margaret Koluccy and her staff were assigned to find artwork and unique craft pieces to decorate the congressional office, including items manufactured in Kansas City. Even though some items may not be deemed as important or impressive to the average visitor, they were extremely important to the manufacturer. Like his employees, Marks wanted the manufacturers to know their work was also important to him.

Marks set a goal of listening to the mind of every congressman in the House. Jerome created a schedule to log interviews of each of the 435 congressional members. Marks wanted to learn their strength and weakness. He wanted leverage, so he could lean on them to vote with him. He did not particularly enjoy digging into people's lives…but he knew that was the way to get bills passed.

Marks purposely became an oddity. He planned to spend almost all his time in the Capitol, sitting in his chair within the House chamber, regardless of what was happening in the chamber. He avoided the interruptions of phone calls, lobbyists, and paperwork in his office; instead, he spent time reading. He heard every speech given by every house member to, most times, a nearly-empty chamber. Marks would seize the opportunity to talk with that member about their speech while listening to their mind. Then, he directed Jerome to check that name off the list.

Marks also started learning how the House did business. Bills were only submitted to the House for debate and then to voting if the committee, under whose egis the bill fell, approved the bill.

So, which committee do I have to first submit my proposed bill to? thought Marks. He determined that the Financial Services Subcommittee on Housing, Community Development, and Insurance made the most sense, as it handled matters involving public, affordable, and rural housing. Marks quickly discovered the need to do something about homelessness was not a new topic. Funding had always been the stumbling block...but he had a radical idea about how to get it.

CHAPTER 3: GLEASON MANSION

Gleason, as the mansion was called, was an extraordinary estate and building, both inside and out. A 12-foot-high fence of native stone enclosed the long, yet narrow 20-acre wooded property. The land sloped up about 150 feet from the front gate toward the back of the lot. A massive steel gate guarded the entrance at the beginning of the winding road that led to Gleason. Ten-foot-tall eagles sculpted in white marble stood on each side of the wooden and polished brass door that was large enough to drive a semi through. They gave a menacing, downward gaze upon those who entered their domain. The entrance opened into an atrium foyer that extended over a hundred feet from the entrance and up three stories to the roof. The atrium roof was covered with various shades of blue glass. The massive room was wide enough to fit a college marching band.

The 70,000-square-foot mansion had four floors, plus a huge underground garage, and mechanical and woodworking shops. The service elevator extended from the garage to the four floors. A separate elevator on the opposite wall of the foyer served the third and fourth floors. The kitchen and servants' quarters, which housed 14 individuals, were on the first floor. The residents lived on the second floor, where there was a long dining room that could seat 30 people, formal parlor to receive guests, den with a gigantic fireplace, office, morning room, living room, recreation room with a billiards table, library with bookshelves covering three walls from floor to ceiling, sunroom, and a poolside patio. The third floor had 15 bedrooms with private bathrooms and a spacious exercise room that overlooked the outdoor pool. The fourth floor had six two-room suites, which is where the Gleason children had lived. All the rooms above the first floor were accessible from the servants' quarters by a labyrinth of narrow passageways built inside the walls, so that servants could come and go to any of the rooms above without being heard or seen. Each room had a concealed wall panel that opened to the passageways. Each room on the third and fourth floors had connecting balconies that allowed quests to look down into the grand foyer.

Gleason sat on the crest of a hill about a mile from the Potomac River. It was built to last a thousand years. A blue tile roof covered the outer masonry and stone walls that were over two feet thick, and the foundation rested on bedrock. Most of the building material was stone, granite, and marble from local quarries. It was constructed at the turn of the 20th century by Charles Gleason, who made his fortune in real estate speculation and development. His successive generations continued to expand the family's wealth. Charles's great-grandson Bruce, the current owner, had four children, all of whom were more interested in spending money than learning the family business. The siblings fought over how much money they would inherit when their father died. After his wife's death, Bruce threw his four offspring out of the mansion and severed their allowance…so they had to go to work. He further distanced himself from them by moving to Europe.

Bruce Gleason and Syntil's Walter Champion were members of the same college fraternity and had remained friends over the years. Champion had been a guest at the mansion several times and was a pallbearer at the funeral of Bruce's wife. When Bruce moved to Europe, he told Champion that he was still welcome to stay at Gleason any time he desired – to just let the butler, Carston, know when he was coming. Six months later, when Marks won the election, Champion asked Bruce if Gloria and Cliff could live there full-time while Cliff was in Congress. Their lawyers wrote a fee-free rental contract to protect both parties, detail the responsibilities of each, and to ensure Bruce's kids could not visit Gleason unless they were invited by the Markses.

The house that Marks's advance house-hunting team of Margaret and Gail recommended was directly behind and one lot to the right of Gleason. Jordan Walker decided to use their suggestion as the security detail quarters.

A banner that read *Welcome, Congressman and Mrs. Marks'* was hung over the front gate when Gloria and Cliff arrived at Gleason. Their security guards, assault weapons slung across their chests, were on duty at the gate. Most of the security detail had arrived a day earlier to do an electronic sweep of Gleason and to inspect the security of the grounds and building. Gloria thought the chief of the security detail would be there to welcome and brief them.

"Where's Crawford?" Gloria asked the guard at the gate.

The guard was embarrassed by the question and shrugged his shoulders. "He took a vacation day, Mrs. Marks. He has some friends here in DC."

Gloria looked at Cliff and shook her head. "Sometimes I wonder about that guy."

Joseph Martin, the estate manager, was standing at the front entrance to Gleason, and escorted them inside. The entire staff was standing in a reception line in the foyer. Martin started making introductions, but Marks surprised them all by introducing Gloria and himself then calling each staff member by name. Marks stumbled when he got to Kate O'Rourke. Her mind was closed to him. Total silence. Marks quickly recovered from this unusual event.

"I apologize, but I don't know your name. It's not on my dance card," smiled Marks.

She grinned in return. "My name is Kate O'Rourke. Mr. Marks, Mrs. Marks, I'm your server in the dining room," she stated and warmly shook their hands.

When the introductions were finished, Gloria asked Carston where everyone could sit while she made some comments.

He led the way to the dining room, which contained an elongated dining table with plenty of space.

"My husband and I are thrilled to be here. Pictures of the mansion don't come close to showing how majestic

Gleason is in real life. We are awed by its beauty. You all have done a wonderful job making it shine. We have no plans of changing the way you function. Having a large staff to do the household and outdoor chores is totally foreign to us. My husband was just elected to Congress, so he'll be busy with his new duties. Please see me if you have any needs or questions. Oh, and breakfast and dinner at 7:00 a.m. and 7:00 p.m. for both of us, if possible," Gloria stated, looking directly at the chef.

"We have a 15-person security detail. There will be two with my husband and myself at all times. One security guard will be stationed at the front gate 24/7 and another will be patrolling the grounds. They're being housed in the home behind Gleason. The four guards coming on duty in the morning will have breakfast with us every morning to discuss security issues. The entire security detail will have breakfast with us every Monday. All of them carry concealed weapons and the exterior guards carry semi-automatic assault rifles. Several attempts have been made on my husband's life, which is the reason for the security guards. The two that are with us now are Alexis Perry and Chad Hyler. The members of the security detail will wear this distinctive pin on their lapel," said Gloria, holding up the pin that Bonneville had designed for the detective agency.

Gloria looked at the butler then the estate manager. "Would you take me on a tour of the living quarters, and my husband on a tour of the garage and the grounds?"

"Yes, ma'am," they replied in unison.

The basement area was enormous. There were stalls for six vehicles, an auto repair shop, and a woodworking shop. Surprisingly, in the far corner, stood a glass-enclosed racquetball court.

Marks gave Martin a puzzled look.

"Mr. Gleason loved to play. His children also played and were exceptionally good, but they could never beat their father."

"Does anyone on the staff play?" asked Marks.

"No one was allowed to when the family lived here and I never changed the policy when they left last year," said Martin.

"Change the policy. In three months, after we have a chance to practice, Gloria, the security guards, and I will challenge the staff in singles and doubles," Marks declared.

Behind the racquetball court, in the dark recesses of the basement, was an enormous steel door. Marks tried opening it, but it was locked.

"I was never given a key to this door," said Martin.

"Strange. For security reasons, I want to know what's behind the door," said Marks. "Get Justin Boyd, the maintenance man, to see if he can open the door."

Boyd appeared with a large circle filled with keys. Surprisingly, it only took him a minute to find the right key.

"Have you ever opened this door?" Marks asked Boyd.

"Just once. I thought maybe it was a bomb shelter from the 1950s. According to a map on the back of the door, it connects to several homes next to Gleason. It's kind of spooky. I didn't know if the place was safe after all these years, so I never explored inside and just kept the door locked."

"Are there lights?" asked Marks.

"Should be."

Boyd reached in and flicked a switch. Some of the overhead lights still worked and partially illuminated a lengthy hallway.

Marks looked at Alexis. "You game for some exploring?"

"Absolutely! You all stay here and I'll recon the place." She used her smartphone to take a photo of the map then headed down the hallway.

"Come find me when you get back. I'll be in one of the shops," said Marks.

Alexis returned to the entrance in 30 minutes, searching for Marks.

"Everything seems safe to me. The walls look and feel like solid concrete. There are two long hallways that lead away from the main complex of 10 rooms. The doors are locked and have addresses on them. One is the address where the security detail lives. The other address is the house next to it. There's furniture and beds in the rooms. I counted 50 single beds," said Alexis, who was clearly excited.

She continued, "This is an amazing place, Mr. Marks. There's a commercial kitchen and a fully stocked china closet. The pantry and cold storage are, of course, empty. There are men's and women's lockers, a recreation room, laundry room, power generator room, and a workshop with tons of hand tools."

"Take Mr. Boyd to those doors to make sure we have the keys. Coming from the security guards' quarters to Gleason through the shelter would be an excellent way to keep a lower profile. But for right now," said Marks, eyeing Boyd and Martin, "not a word to anyone until I have time to sort this out with Jordan Walker. I'm coming, Alexis. Martin, are you game to join?" asked Marks.

"Yes, sir."

———————————

The Markses entered the dining room at 7:00 p.m. Kate O'Rourke was standing by the sideboard, ready to serve.

"What are the ground rules of your duties?" Marks asked the server.

"After you select from the menu at your place setting, I plate the food and serve it until you're satisfied. I bring your meals to you, wherever you are in the house. I stay until you're finished eating, until I'm dismissed, or when you leave the dining room. I clear the table and set it up an hour before the next meal. I bring up the food in the dumbwaiter from the kitchen and lay out the food on the sideboard. Please tell me if there's a meal you'd like, or if there are foods you dislike. If more than six people will be dining, one or both of the maids will help. You'll see both of them when your security team has breakfast on Monday.

More importantly, what I hear here stays here. To not do so is grounds for immediate termination," said O'Rourke.

"I think my adversaries will try to gain intelligence about what goes on in the mansion. They might try to bribe someone on the staff for that intelligence. Since you don't live here, you're more accessible. If they target you, give them what they want to know and charge a high price – but tell us what and who they are."

"Understood, sir."

CHAPTER 4: THE SPY

Gloria and Cliff enjoyed their newfound morning jogging routine. Sometimes, they ran down the driveway toward the main entrance to chat with the guard on duty. One morning, they arrived at the gate just as two female household staff members (who did not live in Gleason) strolled through the front gate. One of the women, Nadine Harrison, smiled and said, "Good morning" to the Markses. The other, Kate O'Rourke, who was typically friendly, kept her head down, averted her eyes, muttered a salutation, and quickly handed Marks a small slip of paper before walking past them toward Gleason.

"What did she give you?" Gloria asked as they continued their jog around the estate's perimeter.

"I still can't listen to her mind," said Marks, frustrated. "She gave me a piece of paper that says, 'Floor plan = $10K.'"

"Wow, $10,000. Wonder who wants a floor plan? What do you mean? You couldn't hear anything in her mind?" inquired Gloria, somewhat amazed.

"No. Remember the first day at Gleason? I didn't know her name. She's the third person whose mind is closed to me. It happened with one of the political staff and one of the congressmen, so it wasn't a big deal," said Marks.

"Why can't you hear them?"

"Must be because my receivers can't turn to the frequency emitted by their brains."

"Why don't you get the engineers at Syntil to find out why?" Gloria suggested.

"Since it only happened a couple times, I didn't think it was worth the trouble…and it wasn't important."

"I think it's worth the trouble. For your security, we need to know as much as we can about the people who have access to our home," said Gloria.

"You're right. I'll call Jordan after breakfast."

"Maybe I should practice what I preach, and interview all of the staff members. So far, I've just let the estate manager run the staff," said Gloria.

"How much do we pay them?" asked Cliff.

"I don't know. Guess I opened my big mouth preaching to you and stepped on my tongue in the process. I'll do a complete human resource review of every aspect of the entire staff," said Gloria.

Marks called Jordan Walker after breakfast to explain the challenge of not being able to hear certain people's minds.

"The engineers are aware of the problem; it was such a rare occurrence that we didn't see the need to spend any resources to fix the problem. But since this is the third event, this goes beyond an anomaly – there will probably be more. It's time to address the problem. I'll talk with the Project Deuces manager and get an engineer assigned to find a solution. Okay, Cliff?"

"Thanks, Jordan. Talk to you later."

The next phone call was to Bonneville Taylor. "Hey, Cliff. What's going on?" he asked.

"I need your help. I want you to send a couple of our field investigators to DC. I want to do an in-depth background check on one of the household staff members. The young woman's name is Kate O'Rourke. She's about 5 feet, 6 inches; in her late 20s; and has red hair and freckles. Her mind is completely closed to me. I have no idea what she's thinking, except that she slipped me a note that said she'll receive $10,000 from someone by providing them a floor plan of Gleason. She doesn't live at the mansion. That's all I know about her. Gloria's going to do a complete profile on the entire staff. She may need additional help, but for now, just concentrate on O'Rourke. I want to know who's willing to pay her to spy on us."

"Wow, that's a first," Bonneville replied.

"Not really, but this time, it's important. If the agency has some field investigators to spare, I want them to do a background check of O'Rourke and find out who wanted her to provide them with a floor plan of the mansion."

"I'll have two people on a flight this afternoon. Who do I bill for the time and expenses?"

"Me," said Cliff.

———————————————

Using data from Martin's payroll files, his personal knowledge of the staff members, and her interviews with staffers, Gloria put together file folders for each employee.

1. Joseph Martin, Estate Manager. *Sixty-two years old; 6 feet, 2 inches. A retired sergeant major with 25 years in the Marines. Employed by Gleason for the past eight years. Salary: $75,000 a year with three weeks' vacation. Overall management of the estate; has hiring and firing authority. The maintenance and outdoor staff report to him. Approves all purchase invoices, sets the pay scale, and disburses weekly wages. Responsible for a $3 million annual budget. Lives in Gleason.*

2. Robert Carston, Butler. *Age: 58, 6 feet 2 inches tall, and in excellent condition. Has been employed at Gleason for 12 years. Annual salary is $65,000. Worked in England as a butler. Mr. Gleason had seen Carston in one of the royal family's homes during his travels and instantly liked him. He offered Carston a $20,000 bonus if he came to work at his home. Overall responsible for the daily operations of the interior staff. Reports to the residents, Cliff and Gloria Marks. Gets three weeks' vacation and lives in Gleason.*

3. Mary Tanner, Housekeeper. *Fifty-two years old; 5 feet, 8 inches. Has been employed at Gleason for 10 years. Has a background of working on cruise ships. Annual salary is $55,000 with three weeks' vacation. Responsible for the interior cleanliness of Gleason. Supervises three maids. She has a room in Gleason; on weekends, she stays at her son's home in Arlington, Virginia.*

4. Fred Beck, Chef. *Forty-six years old and 5 feet, 4 inches tall. Employed at Gleason for the past six years. Salary is $55,000 per year with two weeks' vacation. Spent 20 years working in* numerous restaurant kitchens. Responsible for buying food products and food preparation. Supervises the sous-chef and one kitchen helper. Lives at Gleason.

5. Clint Browning, Master Gardener/Landscaper. Fifty-two years old; 5 feet, 10 inches. Has been a Gleason employee for 10 years. Makes $58,000 a year. Supervises the full-time groundskeeper and is authorized to hire additional seasonal help. Lives at Gleason.

6. Jeb Winters, Groundskeeper. Age: 31; 5 feet, 11 inches. Employed at Gleason for the past eight years. Salary is $45,000 per year with two weeks' vacation. Lives at Gleason.

7. Justin Boyd, Electrical and Mechanical Maintenance. Forty-eight years old; 6 feet, 1 inch tall. Employed at Gleason for 14 years. Annual salary is $60,000 with three weeks' vacation. Supervises woodcraftsman and handyman/general laborer. Lives in childhood home in Georgetown.

8. Kate O'Rourke, Dining Room Server. Twenty-seven years old; 5 feet, 6 inches tall. Employed at Gleason for two years. Salary is $35,000 per year with two weeks' vacation. Lives in Alexandria, Virginia.

9. Sue Proulx, Maid. Twenty-eight years old; 5 feet, 6 inches. Has been employed at Gleason for five years. Salary is $37,000 with two weeks' vacation. Primarily responsible for 15 bedrooms on the second floor.

10. Beth Sounder, Maid. Twenty-six years old; 5 feet, 5 inches tall. Employee of Gleason for four years. Annual salary is $36,000 with two weeks' vacation. Primarily responsible for the main living area.

11. *Nadine Harrison, Maid.* *Twenty-nine years old and 5 feet, 9 inches tall. Employed at Gleason for the past five years. Salary is $37,000 per year with two weeks' vacation. Responsible for the four two-rooms suites/kitchenettes on the fourth floor. Lives with ailing mother in Alexandria, Virginia.*

12. *Rino Carver, Sous-Chef.* *Age: 32; 5 feet, 10 inches. Has been a Gleason employee for six years. Annual salary is $48,000 with three weeks' vacation. Lives in McLean, Virginia. He has an evening job at a local restaurant.*

13. *Seth Dickerson, Woodcraftsman.* *Twenty-eight years old and an even six feet tall. Employed at Gleason for the past seven years. Salary is $49,000 with three weeks' vacation. Lives in Gleason.*

14. *Robert Kasman, Handyman/General Laborer.* *Thirty years old and has been employed at Gleason for eight years. Annual salary is $40,000 with two weeks' vacation. Lives in Gleason.*

After running some numbers, Gloria calculated the total annual salary for Gleason's 14 employees to be $695,000. She was surprised at the cumulative amount, yet disappointed that the paid vacation was the only benefit offered.

Martin got bent out of shape when Gloria began firing off questions about the employees.

"Why are you concerned about the costs and benefits?" the estate manager asked, seemingly annoyed, perhaps anxious.

"Obviously, Mr. Gleason didn't tell you that my husband is responsible for the salaries of the staff, including yours. He deposits the money into the account that you draw the salaries from. Mr. Gleason pays for major repairs and equipment for the estate, property taxes, and insurance. My husband also pays the utility bills, minor repairs, plus food and supplies. Mr. Gleason agreed to go halves with me on the cost of expanding the pool to 50 meters in length, which will cost about 150 grand. It's our intent to buy the Gleason estate upon his death, or sooner, if he so chooses. He's included an option in his will that states we have the first option to buy the estate at market price; all proceeds would go to his children and his charities. From what I've heard, none of his kids could afford the upkeep of the Gleason, let alone the employees' salaries. Secondly, there are people who wish to do harm to my husband because of the enemies his detective agency has made. There have been several lethal attempts, which is why we now have full-time security guards. I want to make sure no one can go through the staff to get to me or my husband. Certainly you can understand that's why I want happy, loyal employees," Gloria stated.

"I stand corrected, Mrs. Marks. I totally understand your position. What would you like me to do?" asked Martin.

"What *can* we do to improve their loyalty?" Gloria replied.

"Medical health insurance would be great," said Martin.

"I anticipated that. I've done some back-of-the-envelope calculations and I think we can get excellent coverage for $90,000 a year. I'll call our personal attorney to make it happen. He'll be calling you to get information on the staff. What else?" she asked.

"The salaries have been constant for the past five years."

"I was thinking of a 10% increase for everyone. It looks like you only increased salaries based upon the number of years someone's worked here. Make sure the base salaries have increased $1,000 per year for every year over three years. Fairness helps in the loyalty column," said Gloria.

"When do you want the pay increases to start?"

"This week's paycheck – not prorated, but for the full week. Also, please tell the staff they should be able to have medical coverage in a couple weeks or sooner. The coverage is for family and dependents, such as Nadine's mother. The insurance agency will ask them a lot of questions. Anything else, Mr. Martin?"

"No, ma'am," replied Martin.

"I have two more items. For your information only, my husband's detective agency is doing an extensive background investigation on Kate O'Rourke to find out about the people who contacted her," said Gloria.

"Why Kate O'Rourke?"

"She's been offered 10 grand to provide a floor plan of Gleason," replied Gloria.

"Who would want the floor plan – burglars?" asked Martin.

31

"That's my guess, but my husband's detective agency will find out who wants it. I'll let you know what they uncover. Moving on. One last item on my list: Have the maids and servers brainstorm to come up with a better-looking uniform – one that signifies they work at Gleason. The same goes for the rest of the staff."

"Yes, ma'am."

"You may have doubts that I know what I'm doing," Gloria paused and continued to hold Martin's eye contact. "I was the administrative director of a large hospital, so dealing with this small staff shouldn't be a monumental task to handle."

Five days after Marks called the detective agency about a background investigation on Kate O'Rourke, he had their report.

O'Rourke was 27 years old and was born and raised in Alexandria, Virginia. Her father died five years ago in an auto accident. Her mother become chronically ill and had to move in with Kate. She had a stack of medical bills for her mother's medical care, which forced her to quit college and get a job. Kate O'Rourke had to quit several jobs due to bouts of urinary infection. Two years ago, she applied to work at Gleason because it was an easy commute from her apartment and free meals were part of the pay. With her college loan and medical bills, she was $90,000 in debt.

Her credit cards, which were maxed out until recently, were paid off two weeks ago. She then began making payments on the medical bills.

Her sudden source of new wealth came with the appearance of two men. Video surveillance cameras in the apartment complex showed images of both men and their rental car. The rental car contract provided a name and address in Texas. Internet investigation revealed that the Texas men worked for Houston Electronic and Advanced Technology. They told O'Rourke they were gathering information to write a book about Cliff Marks. From his humble beginnings to now living in the Gleason was almost a magical rise to fame. She was offered $10,000 to draw an outline of Gleason's interior floor plan. She took the money to pay back rent to avoid getting evicted from their apartment. The two men came again a week later, offering another $10,000 to plant some devices in Gleason in order to learn more about the current residents. She was also given an iPhone to take pictures of the interior. They assured her they meant no harm to anyone and were not thieves.

O'Rourke's mother told a neighbor lady that the two men were freelance writers who were doing a series of magazine articles on servants and their employers. The men gave her daughter $20,000 and promised more money, depending on how much information she could provide them. The neighbor thought the mother was bragging and that the two men were probably bill collectors.

The neighbor lady had heard Kate make bitter remarks about being a servant. Her mother said she took the job because it was easy work and the home was beautiful. She liked the other employees, especially the estate manager. She hoped he would make a pass at her to get leverage for a pay raise. More importantly, it gave her access to health food that she pilfered from the kitchen pantry at Gleason, which saved them a lot of money. Kate brought home a bag filled with food almost every day.

The report contained two photos of the men from Texas.

Marks guessed the men's next request would be the codes to disarm the home's security system. He wanted her to give them the codes. He could capture the men *inside* the Gleason mansion.

The next morning, Marks came down for breakfast 15 minutes early. He quietly looked into the dining room and saw Kate O'Rourke pacing the width of the dining room as if she were trying to figure out its dimensions.

"It's 46 feet wide and 65 feet long," said Marks.

O'Rourke was startled, but said nothing. She quickly resumed her position at the sideboard that was lined with heated serving dishes of breakfast food.

"Hashbrown potatoes, scrambled eggs, biscuits with sausage gravy, coffee with two Splendas and two creams, if you would, please," said Marks. He laid the two photos of the men from Texas on the table next to his place setting.

O'Rourke filled a plate with food and placed it in front of Marks, along with a small slip of paper. She paused for a second when she saw the photos then murmured, "Yes."

While Marks was eating, his personal two-person security detail for the day and the two security guards responsible for the front gate and exterior of the estate joined him for breakfast.

Marks passed the photos across the table to his personal security detail.

"Sir, do you think they're a threat?"

"Possibly. Houston Electronic and Advanced Technology's last attempt to kidnap me failed, and when six of their people were killed, their CEO declared a permanent truce. Gloria's traveling to Houston to have a chat with the CEO. These two men could be in town for business," said Marks.

A minute after Marks walked inside Gleason, he knew something was wrong. He felt the same sensation in his implant as when he discovered the planted camera and microphone in Stu Nichols's apartment. Marks found Gloria and quietly pressed her to put on gym clothes to join him for a pre-dinner jog. As they trotted down the road to the guard station at the estate's entrance, Marks told Gloria that listening devices had been planted in Gleason. Upon arriving at the guard station, they, along with the security guard, looked through the entry logbook. Gloria pointed to one of the entries that read, 'Flyover by small drone'. It was dated three days ago, but mentioned nothing else. No service or maintenance crew had entered. One of the young maids, who lived with her ailing mother, had come and gone, as well as Kate O'Rourke.

"I think there's been a security breach. I want an electronic sweep done tonight after the staffers go to bed – the dining room, den, living room, our bedrooms, gym, and bathrooms. These are the rooms that the maids know we use. Find the devices, but don't remove them," Gloria instructed.

She always had an edge in her voice when she addressed the security staff. She wanted them to know their job was serious business and not some easy gig. They knew that she was not a person to be taken lightly; she had demonstrated several times that she was afraid of no one. Gloria knew their job could be boring and tedious at times, so it was good to have an issue to spark their interest.

Gloria and Cliff stayed up late that night watching a movie on the large TV in the den until the security staff did the electronic sweep. They limited their conversation to ordinary husband-and-wife chatter.

The following day, Gloria and Alexis used the underground tunnel for the first time to travel undetected to the staff house to talk with Crawford, the head of the security detail.

Crawford stood and offered the chair at his desk to Gloria as she walked into his office. Gloria said nothing until she sat down.

"I want to see the background files on the household staff at Gleason," Gloria insisted.

"I don't have any background files," replied Crawford.

"Let me get this straight…you guard the front door, but leave the back door wide open. Why is that?"

"I was never told to do background checks, and secondly, it's not part of my job description. I was hired to supervise the security detail that provides personal protection for you and your husband, not to go poking around into people's lives. Personally, I find that sort of thing distasteful," said Crawford, with a trace of 'Gotcha' in his voice. He had always privately scoffed at having to take directions from this woman – or any woman, for that matter – but the pay was great and the job was easy.

"Goddamn it," she said, slamming the palm of her hand on the desktop.

Crawford was startled. He had never heard Gloria swear before.

"I want you to get started immediately doing background checks on all the Gleason staffers," directed Gloria.

"I'll check with Jordan Walker to see if he wants them done," said Crawford.

"You don't need to check with anybody. *I'm* telling you to do them."

"Mrs. Marks, I don't work for you." His face was flushed. He was having a hard time controlling the anger in his voice.

"Crawford, your attitude pisses me off. You work at the pleasure of me and my husband. You can pack your bags and go back to Kansas City," Gloria said, as she stood and pointed her index finger at Crawford.

"You don't have the authority to fire me," Crawford defiantly replied while pointing his finger back at her.

By now, Alexis had slowly moved closer to Crawford and was watching his every move.

"Watch carefully," Gloria instructed. She pulled out her cell phone and called Jordan Walker.

The Syntil operation center answered the phone.

"Mrs. Marks, this is Phil Hillsborough at the operation center. Jordan Walker is offline today."

"Okay. Can you patch me through to Lance Winford?"

"Yes, ma'am."

"Gloria, good to hear your voice. What's going on?" Winford asked warmly.

Gloria relayed her conversation with Crawford. She also expressed his opinion to Winford that he did not work for her and Cliff, and they did not have the authority to fire him.

"Technically, he's right...but from a practical standpoint, he's dead wrong. Is he with you now?"

"Yes," said Gloria, before handing the phone to Crawford. The conversation was one-sided, with the CEO of Syntil doing all the talking. Crawford's frustration mounted as he made several attempts to get in the dialogue, but without success.

The conversation ended with, "Yes, sir."

"You bitch," Crawford yelled, hurling the phone at Gloria.

Gloria caught the phone in her hand before the well-aimed missile struck her in the face.

Alexis knocked Crawford to the floor with a sweeping forearm blow across his chest. She was straddling his body with her legs. She hoped he would fight back.

"Let him up, Alexis. Escort him to his room, so he can pack his bags. Take his security entry card then have a guard take him to the airport and make sure he gets on a flight to Kansas City," Gloria ordered.

Gloria informed Cliff of the day's events when he arrived home from work. They went to a spare bedroom on the third floor – a place where Cliff knew there were no listening devices. She shared her disappointment about the conversation with Crawford. Cliff agreed that their first action was to improve the employment benefits of the household staff.

"I think we should get Buhrowe involved to help us decide what to do, especially with the employment contracts," said Cliff.

"I'm ready to call him right now," Gloria replied, still worked up from her meeting with Crawford.

"Call him," Cliff urged, pulling the phone number from his implant's memory.

"Buhrowe."

"Gloria Marks here."

"Hey, beautiful. Nice to hear your voice! Is this social or business?"

"We need your help. The employment contracts and benefits for the household staff that we took over from the owner are relics. Could you come to Washington and put things in order?"

"Sure. I can come out tomorrow. I'll bring my secretary with me. Sounds like there may be a lot of paperwork to generate," said Buhrowe.

"You can stay with us. There's a ton of room for you both. I'll have the staff set up an office for you," said Gloria.

"Looking forward to seeing you and Cliff. Bye," he replied before hanging up.

The following afternoon, Carston asked Gloria for a meeting with Mr. Marks when he returned from the Capitol.

Carston entered their office, which was located next to the den. Kate O'Rourke was with him.

"This is a very unpleasant situation to report. Young Kate has fallen prey to two shysters. They somehow discovered her serious financial situation, and how she and her mother were about to be evicted from Kate's apartment. They offered her large sums of money for information about Gleason and the two of you. They told her they were writing a book about American servants and their employers. When she overheard your conversation with the security guards at breakfast and saw the photos of the two men, she knew there was a more serious game afoot than some magazine or book. She then came to me."

"Mr. Marks, I'm so sorry," she said, tears welling up in her eyes.

"Thank you, Kate...but you had no way of knowing. Your notes to me have been helpful. Gloria and I weren't always rich, so we understand the financial pressure you were under with your mother's poor health. We want you to continue providing the two men with any information they want. Bargain for as much money as you can. We suspect they'll hire accomplices to enter Gleason one night to kidnap me or Gloria. With your help, we'll be waiting for them. Alexis Perry, the head of our security guards, will speak with you. Keep her informed at all times, day or night, as this situation continues to unfold," said Marks.

Two days later, a note accompanied Cliff's breakfast menu. It read:

The security codes to the alarm system were worth $20K. – KO

Starting that evening, a guard, equipped with night vision goggles, was positioned on top of Gleason, looking down on the backyard of the house. The logical way for an intruder to gain entry into the house was over the back fence and across the patio. The security panel by the back door could silence the alarm system before they scaled the wall of Gleason and crawled into the empty bedroom next to the Markses' bedroom.

At night, four bodyguards were concealed in the hallway (two at each end) to contain intruders if they appeared in the hallway. Everyone was in radio contact with the rooftop guard. Three days later, at 2:00 a.m., two intruders dressed in black and wearing night vision goggles, climbed over the stone wall behind Gleason. The security guard in charge of patrolling the exterior of the mansion was warned to stay away from the back of the mansion. Marks wanted to capture the intruders, not scare them away.

The ledges on the mansion's walls enabled the experienced climbers to quickly scale the house. They crawled through the window of the bedroom next to the Markses', where they attached a steel cable to the window ledge that led back to a tree outside the stone fence. The ripline could be used for their own (and possibly, a restrained victim's) escape from the mansion.

Just before the intruders clambered over the stone wall, the rooftop sentry spotted them and let out a warning. Gloria and Cliff stepped from their bedroom and into the dark hallway with the bodyguards. Another guard was in the passageway within Gleason's walls. He moved to the bedroom the intruders used for entry; as soon as the intruders appeared in the hallway, he entered the bedroom through the concealed wall panel and locked the door.

They heard the bedroom door open then quietly close behind them. Silence.

"Welcome to Gleason," Marks said, as the hallway lights turned on.

"Are you looking for us?" asked Gloria from the other end of the long hallway.

The two men tried going back into the bedroom, but the door was locked. They frantically started checking other doors as the Markses and their bodyguards started closing in on them. Mistakenly, the utility room door was not locked. The utility room housed a dumbwaiter that led to the laundry room in the basement. The two intruders managed to cram themselves into the dumbwaiter and were out of sight by the time the bodyguards checked the utility room. Marks radioed to the exterior guard to intercept them in the basement.

Leaving one guard behind to guard the dumbwaiter, the rest of them hurried to the service elevator and headed for the basement.

"They're in a car," radioed the exterior guard. "Front gate, raise the barriers!"

As the service elevator door opened into the basement, they heard the squeal of tires. A car sped out of the basement and made the sharp left turn onto the driveway.

"No shooting," radioed Marks.

The car was no match for the four cylindrical steel-and-concrete barriers that rose from the earth to block the front gate. The driver swerved to the left and missed slamming the car broadside into the barriers by mere inches. The front gate guard had the intruders handcuffed and on the ground before Marks and Gloria, along with the other security guards that were with them in the mansion, arrived at the gate.

Marks listened to their minds. "Ten grand apiece for a day's work…right, Tom?" asked Marks.

Silence.

"So, Everett. What did you think your benefactors were going to do with us once we were delivered to them?" Gloria asked, eyeing the other man.

Silence.

"How did a couple of mountain climbers like you two get involved in a kidnapping scheme with the two Texas men? What do you suppose the Texans will do when you don't show up at the airport on time?" Marks inquired.

"I know!" Gloria answered. "They're going to abandon the RV they rented to transport us back to Texas and use the airline tickets they were going to give you then leave town with your 20 grand."

The silence was finally broken. "How did you know we were coming?" Tom asked.

"The better question is – what are we going to do with you two?" asked Marks, intimidatingly.

One of the intruder's cell phones chimed – a new text message. *'What's your status?'*

Gloria texted back *'On our way'* from the intruder's phone.

"Take the handcuffs off," ordered Marks. "This is your lucky day, fellows. But if we see you again, it'll be your last day. Hit the road."

After the intruders walked through the gate and down the road, Marks told Gloria, "I didn't want to turn them over to the police. They'd ask a lot of questions. Who knows what our visitors would say? And I don't want this in the newspaper."

Cliff used his tactical radio to call the rooftop lookout. "Come on down. The fun is over," he directed.

"Good teamwork, everyone!" Gloria said to the four security personnel as she shook their hands.

CHAPTER 5: BRINGING THE HEAT

"HEAT Corporation, how can I direct your call?"

"Mr. Gordan's office, please," Gloria replied.

"One moment."

After a brief pause, a voice said, "Mr. Gordan's office."

"Hi, I'm an old college classmate of Jimmy's. I'm going to be in Houston tomorrow and wanted to stop by and say hi. Will he be working tomorrow?" asked Gloria.

"He has a busy schedule tomorrow. Can I tell him who's calling?"

"Oh, I want to surprise him. Thanks! Bye."

―――――――――――

At 9:00 a.m. the following morning, Gloria and Alexis arrived in the main lobby of the HEAT headquarters in Houston.

"How can I help you?" asked the receptionist.

"Would you tell Jim Gordan that Gloria Marks is here and wants a minute of his time?" said Gloria.

"Do you have an appointment?"

"No, but I'm sure he'll see me. I know Jim will be angry if he found out I was here and nobody told him. You're new here…and I just don't want you to get in trouble, sweetie," Gloria answered, flashing a smile.

A minute later, the receptionist had the CEO on the other end of the line.

"What does this woman look like?" asked Gordan.

"Thick, beautiful, dark hair and very attractive, sir."

"Is anyone with her?"

"Yes, sir. Another woman."

"Alert security. Tell Mrs. Marks that I'll be right down."

Alexis noticed two company security guards enter the lobby then join another standing at the front entrance.

"Do you know who that woman is?" asked one guard.

"No, why should I?"

"She's the bitch who put two of our guys in the hospital when they tried to grab her at the Kansas City International Airport. I'm not going anywhere near her for what they're paying me."

By then, Alexis had whispered in Gloria's ear. Gloria turned, looked at the three guards, and smiled. She flexed her index finger at them to invite them over.

The biggest of the three guards approached Gloria and Alexis, but stayed 10 feet away from them.

"We come in peace. You behave and I'll behave, alright?" Gloria promised.

"Yes, ma'am."

"Are your friends out of the hospital?" she asked.

"Yes, ma'am," he replied before rejoining the other guards at the front entrance.

Moments later, Jim Gordan stepped out of the elevator with two security guards, who both stopped when they spotted Gloria. Gordan hesitated for a second then continued across the lobby to Gloria.

"Mrs. Marks, I hope you and your husband are well," said Gordan, as he extended his right hand.

"That all depends," Gloria responded, taking his hand, but not letting go. "Two of your people came to DC and bribed one of my household staff members to provide information about our home. Then, they hired two men to break into our home to kidnap my husband and me. They failed."

"Believe me, I knew nothing about this. Who are the two men from HEAT?" asked Gordan.

Alexis opened a folder and removed the photo of both men. She handed it to Gloria, who let go of Gordan's hand to pass him the photo.

"I don't know them. Let me take you to our Human Resources department to verify they work for the company."

The HR boss called in their personnel manager, who was startled to see the CEO in their office.

After studying the photo, she said, "Yes, sir. Both of these men work for the company."

"Have them report to my office," directed the HR boss. "Use my phone."

Gloria and Alexis moved across the room, so people would not notice them when they entered the office.

"Who are they?" asked Gordan.

"They work in our security office for material classification and proprietary information."

When the two men walked into the HR office and saw the CEO, they feared the worst.

"Were you two in DC this past week?" Gordan inquired.

They sheepishly nodded their heads.

"On company business? And if so, who sent you there and for what purpose?"

"Your executive assistant, Sid James. He gave us $250,000 for the project."

"Project? Project!?" yelled Gordan. "Is that what you call kidnapping? That son of a bitch! Now I know why he quit yesterday. He was freelancing while I was gone on the cruise with Captain Blackman," said Gordan, glancing at Gloria.

One of the two men, Ted Nelsen, suddenly grew a backbone and spoke up. "He said the company failed, so he was going to try."

"Yes, I failed because I trusted someone who went way, way beyond my plan to discover the new technology Syntil had developed. It wasn't my intention to fire missiles at a mega-yacht, or for six bodies to end up at the bottom of the sea and two more seriously injured. She warned me that if it happened again, she'd come back and kill someone – probably me. The only reason she didn't kill you," Gordan explained through glares, "is because she wanted to find out if I broke my promise and whose idea this project was."

He stopped then asked, "Where's James?"

"We went to his apartment last night to tell him what happened and give back the money we didn't spend. His apartment was empty. We returned the money to finance this morning," Nelsen stated.

"Tell finance to come here," Gordan told the HR boss.

Ned Bailey, the finance director, appeared in the doorway and reported, "Yes, sir. Nelsen returned $180 grand this morning. It was a very unusual transaction. I gave them the $250,000 because James said you authorized it. I tried to call you, sir, but you were out of town. I could dock his final paycheck to recoup some of the $70,000 that was lost. I informed him that his check wouldn't be ready until tomorrow. He was upset, but I explained how we had to validate his vacation time, sick leave pay, any severance pay, and the value of his stock options."

"He'll still be in town to get his paycheck. Let me know when he comes to pick it up tomorrow," said Gordan.

Gloria looked at Nelsen. "Where do you think he's holed up?"

"I don't know where he's staying, but I do know he likes The Horizon Bar. That's where we got to know him. We checked to see if he was there last night. The hostess said we just missed him."

"Alexis and I will find him. You better get with your lawyers, Gordan, to see what kind of settlement you want to offer to compensate for home invasion and attempted kidnapping. You got away pretty cheap the first time," Gloria said before she and Alexis left the corporate headquarters.

After stopping for lunch and discussing their plan to approach Sid James, they drove to The Horizon Bar. They arrived at the bar at 2:00 p.m. Gloria went in by herself and asked the bartender, Candy, if she knew Sid James. She did.

Gloria continued by stating James owed her $2,000. She offered Candy $100 to call her when he showed up and another $100 when Gloria reentered the bar. Gloria left her phone number with Candy then walked outside to join Alexis in their car parked across the street. Then, they waited. After about an hour, Alexis went inside the bar. She drank beer and did shots while chatting up the bartender and playing with her smartphone.

"Some of the guys at HEAT said that Sid James hung out here," Alexis casually mentioned.

"Does he owe you money, too?"

"No, no. Besides being hot, he does make a ton of money."

"You know how much?" Candy asked, as she stopped working, walked over to Alexis, put her elbows on the bar, and leaned toward Alexis.

"Two hundred thousand plus bonuses," Alexis responded.

"That cheap bastard! I was lucky to get a buck tip out of him," said Candy, jerking the bar towel off her shoulder and slamming it on the bar.

"He may be in a peck of trouble. Ned Bailey, the finance director at HEAT, told his staff that James took $250,000 from HEAT without proper authorization. He lied to Bailey that the CEO had approved it."

"I hope he is."

Alexis was working on her third beer and was sitting at the far end of the bar, talking with other customers, when James appeared with another man that looked like a bouncer. They took seats at the bar.

Candy ignored them and used her cell phone. A minute later, Gloria came into the bar. James saw her reflection in the mirror behind the bar.

"That's her," James said to the bouncer-looking man with him. Both men slipped off the stool and faced Gloria. "Get her," whispered James.

The bouncer rushed toward Gloria, hoping to catch her by surprise. He was not fast enough. Gloria sidestepped then tripped the bouncer as he moved past her. She slammed him on his back with her forearm, sending him sprawling on the floor. Just in time, she saw James grab a barstool and throw it at her. Gloria caught the stool in midair, spun it 360 degrees, and threw it back at him. The stool hit him across the chest and knocked him against the bar. James kicked the stool aside and approached Gloria. In an effort to purposely break his jaw, she hit him on the side of his face with a clenched fist. His head lurched to one side, rendering him unconscious. James sunk to the floor as his leg collapsed. By then, the bouncer was on his feet. He lunged at Gloria, but Alexis joined the fight. She grabbed the bouncer by the back of his collar and jerked him off his feet and onto his back. Gloria dropped on his chest with both knees, knocking the wind out of him. Alexis was kneeling on his outstretched arms.

"You want to go another round?" Alexis asked the bouncer.

"No," he whispered, struggling to catch his breath.

After several minutes, the two women helped him to his feet and sat him in a booth.

Someone in the bar had called 911.

Gloria and Alexis were sitting in the booth with the bouncer and having a drink when the police arrived.

"What happened here, Candy?" demanded the officer, who was pointing at James, lying on the floor.

Candy knew all the police in this precinct; they came for free drinks or to break up fights.

"He slipped off the barstool and hit the side of his face. I think his jaw is broken. I heard something crack," lied Candy.

No one else in the bar said a word nor did the police suspect they would. This was Candy's bar.

Five minutes later, an ambulance arrived and loaded the still-unconscious James onto a stretcher and drove away. They, too, had experienced The Horizon Bar before.

On the bar in front of Candy, Gloria laid down three hundred-dollar bills and her Gleason address card.

"If you're ever in the nation's capital city, stop by for a drink," Gloria said, winking. "I'll show you a good time."

"I'll bet you will," replied Candy. She knew exactly what Gloria meant.

CHAPTER 6: BAR FIGHT

Gloria and Cliff had a date to meet at a local steakhouse for drinks and fine dinner of aged beef. Gloria was early, so she took a seat at a small table in the bar area. Most of the patrons in the bar were on their third drink when she arrived, increasing the activity and noise levels. She quickly realized that it was not a place to come to alone, especially at this time of day. She was about to leave when an older man at a nearby table turned and put his hand on her thigh. At first, her bodyguard, who was standing across the crowded room, did not see the man put his hand on Gloria's thigh. When he finally did, Gloria had already responded.

"Hey, sweetie. Can I buy you a drink?"

"No, and take your hand off my leg," she quickly replied.

"Oh, come on, honey," he said, moving closer.

"Last warning. Take your hand off my leg!"

"What are you going to do if I…?"

He never had a chance to say more. Gloria grabbed his hand from her leg and twisted it in a very painful finger submission hold.

The man yelled in pain, falling off his chair and onto his knees.

One on the man's companions grabbed Gloria's neck from behind and shouted over the noise of the crowd, "Let go of him!"

"You guys can't keep your hands to yourself. Let go of me or you're going to end up on the floor next to your buddy," Gloria ordered.

"Fat chance, bitch," were his last words before he hit the floor.

Gloria released the first drunk's hand then turned quickly to her right, where the second drunk was standing, striking him in the ribs with the point of her elbow. She knew the blow had broken several of ribs and knocked the wind out of him. He staggered for a moment. He hung onto a chair and lowered himself to his knees, wincing in agony and gasping for air.

The throng of people at the tables around Gloria were now on their feet and had moved back several feet, not wanting any of part of this one-sided fight. The bar manager and a bouncer made their way through the crowd, just as Gloria was coolly taking a sip of her drink.

"What's going on?" asked the manager, scanning the scene for answers.

Gloria said nothing. Her bodyguard had finally worked his way through the crowded bar and now stood beside her.

"They got touchy-feely with the wrong person," volunteered a member of the crowd. "This one needs to see a doctor," he continued, pointing to the second man on his knees.

Gloria's cell phone beeped to announce Cliff's arrival. She finished her drink and left the bar area to meet him. The group parted as she and her guard walked through them to the dining room.

Cliff knew what happened to Gloria shortly after they were shown to their table.

"You have fun in the bar?" asked Cliff.

"You know I did," said Gloria with a smile.

"I also know that regardless of how much you enjoy and get a thrill from these fights, someday, you may get yourself in over your head and your bodyguard will have to save your ass...if it's not too late."

"That's why I like to practice. But you're right, I may come up against someone that's sober and ready to fight. I'll be more careful, Cliff," she said.

"I'm sure a video of the fight will be downloaded from the bar's surveillance cameras and posted on Facebook and YouTube within the hour. Your fight might even make the local evening news if they find out you're married to a congressman. On top of that possibility, someone may connect you with your fight at the Kansas City International Airport," said Cliff.

While eating their meal, the restaurant manager approached Cliff and Gloria's table and asked if he could join them. Cliff nodded his head and made a motion toward an empty chair.

"I want to apologize for what happened, Miss…" the manager's words trailed off.

"No need to apologize. I realized shortly after I came into the bar that it was the wrong time to be there," said Gloria, not offering her name.

"I can see the bruise on your neck. Would you let the paramedic examine you before they leave? They just finished loading the drunk with the painful ribs into one of the ambulances. The one with the sore hand declined treatment," said the manager.

"For insurance and liability?" asked Cliff. He saw two paramedics standing at the entrance of the dining room.

"Yes, sir."

Cliff motioned to the paramedics. They came over to their table and escorted Gloria to the ambulance to do a physical assessment for any injuries. Twenty minutes later, Gloria entered the restaurant with her left arm in a cloth sling. A new, complimentary meal and a fresh Jack Daniel's and water was served upon her return. She took a big swig of the drink before sitting down.

"How did it go?" Cliff asked.

"I'm going to have a hell of a sore elbow and a technicolor bruise."

"Nothing broken?"

"Not in their opinion, but they advised me to go to an immediate care facility to have my elbow X-rayed. The HIPPA laws prohibit the paramedics from telling me about the drunk I poked in the ribs, but I got the impression they were amazed by the damage my elbow did to him. Think we should go find out how he's doing?" inquired Gloria.

"What do you want, a battle damage assessment?" said Cliff, grinning.

"I suppose, just for future reference...so I don't permanently injure someone."

"Okay, finish your dinner, we'll get your elbow X-rayed, then we'll find your wounded saloon warrior. This'll be our entertainment for the evening," said Cliff.

Gloria's elbow was not broken, but she had a bone bruise that would take several months to heal. Cliff told her she was on the injured reserve list from any street fighting.

After several phone calls and a scan by his implant of nearby ERs and hospitals, Cliff located the wounded warrior at a nearby hospital. Although the Markses considered waiting until the victim had totally sobered up to pay him a visit, they decided to go to the hospital instead.

After reading the incident report filed by the paramedics and seeing Gloria's arm in a sling, the charge nurse quickly guessed she was the female combatant. Additionally, the nurse had seen the bar fight online and easily recognized Gloria. Without asking any questions, she led Gloria and Cliff to the wounded warrior's room.

"You didn't hear this from me. He's heavily sedated, so you won't be able to talk with him. He just got out of surgery that closed that hole in his lung and restored his three broken ribs. Congratulations on teaching this bully a lesson," said the nurse.

"Guess I can come back tomorrow to see him?" Gloria asked.

"No hurry. Most likely, he's not going anywhere for a week. Come back in three or four days. I'll tell him that you and your husband dropped by to see him, if that's okay, Mrs. Marks?" asked the nurse.

"Can you tell us who he is?" asked Cliff.

"Sure, he's Gordan McKinney, chief of staff for the Speaker of the House."

"Oh, shit!" said Gloria. "My husband is a House member."

"Super!" said Cliff. "We can use that to our advantage. He's the aggressor; he owes you an apology and many thanks for not filing an assault charge against him."

"Have you met the guy?" Gloria asked.

"No, but I'll be paying him a visit as soon as he returns to work. Can't wait to see the expression on his face when I tell him you're my wife," said Cliff.

"Priceless," said the nurse, just before Gloria did.

Two days later, a dozen roses with a card was delivered to Gleason. The handwritten card had shaky penmanship and stated:

> *Mrs. Marks,*
>
> *Please accept my deepest apology for any harm I may have caused you. I hope you can forgive me for my bad behavior. I'm indebted to you for life.*
>
> *– Gordon McKinney*

Two days after the bar fight, Jerome called.

"Mrs. Marks, this is Jerome. Mr. Marks said I could call you."

"Jerome, you can call me anytime you want, as long as you call me 'Gloria'… and you don't need the pompous congressman's permission. What's up?"

"A man named Fred Tanner called and wanted your phone number. I told him there's not a chance in hell. Then he asked if I'd give you his number."

"Who's Fred Tanner?" asked Gloria.

"He's a liquor salesman. He was in the bar when you took down those two men. He noticed you were drinking whiskey and found out from the bartender that it was Jack Daniel's, which he sells," said Jerome.

"What does he want, my endorsement?"

"More than that, Mrs. Marks…I mean, Gloria. He wants you to make a commercial for Jack Daniel's."

"The guy's been drinking too much of his inventory."

"He didn't sound drunk."

"Why me?"

"He didn't say, but I think you should call him. He said you could make some serious money if the commercial increases sales," Jerome reported.

"Money always gets my attention, Jerome. Okay, call him back and tell him I'll call as soon as I speak with Cliff and our lawyer."

Gloria made $250,000 doing four different commercials about her favorite drink.

CHAPTER 7: HOMELESS BILL

Marks wanted to craft a bill that would recognize homelessness as a national issue. He believed that homelessness was a national disgrace. He wanted the House to establish a standing committee for homelessness, which is now under the House Committee of Financial Service. Many of the past and current efforts have not been able to solve the problem of affordable housing and additional housing due to lack of funding.

Cliff Marks took a radical approach. The American Homelessness Bill required not-for-profit organizations with an operational budget of $5 million or more to contribute 1% of their operating budget to the American Homelessness Agency – that tax would raise over $300 million per year. He knew he would receive a firestorm of protest. He was prepared. Marks countered by proposing to tighten the qualification requirements for 'not-for-profit' status.

His second approach to gain support was to be a pest. He would read the 454 pages of the federal budget, attack each departmental budget, and look for excess and waste. He would keep chipping away at the departments that submitted the budget to the House for approval until they agreed to support his homelessness bill. Marks knew he was the only one with the ability to commit the budget to memory, and to use that ability to fully understand the budgets and where to find surpluses.

Every week, Marks gave a speech on the House floor addressing the metrics of homelessness in one state: how many by age, gender, race, how long, their health, and which part of the state most of them lived in, considering they did not have a roof over their heads. He also showed who and how many were living in their cars, vans, or pickups. Marks alerted particular House members when he planned on giving a speech about their state's homelessness issue. He directed his staff in Kansas City to prepare and ship oversized charts to him that displayed all of these metrics, so he could place them in the aisle next to him when he gave his speech in the House chamber. Marks favored holding a long wooden pointer that he sometimes used to whack the chart to get his audience's attention.

Marks also wanted to change the tax laws to include churches, some of which were rather wealthy and able to give their leaders large salaries and generous benefits. He believed the churches were getting a free ride. They received the same services from the city, state, and federal government as everyone else, but did not have to contribute to the cost. Marks knew it was heresy. As far as he was concerned, the church was just another business – and since the majority of the population was no longer churchgoers, they might support imposing a property tax on church-owned property. And maybe even Sunday's collections. The church provided a service for a fee. If the collection plate ran dry, the church folded, just like any other business. He would use this tactic if he did not gain enough support for the American Homelessness Bill.

Marks's efforts in Kansas City to reduce homelessness were undeniably helpful, yet there was still a long road ahead. His committee was currently negotiating to lease a 300-room hotel that was in bankruptcy if the city would waive property taxes for the first two years.

His committee was also working with an architecture firm. Their goal was to design simple one- and two-bedroom homes (about 700 to 1,000 square feet) with all interior and exterior walls made of concrete block. Steel roofs and rafters could be built on the ground while the walls were being built then lifted into place on the walls. The goal was to construct one of these houses within 30 days.

Rodney Sniff, owner of a 1951 Pontiac Chieftain, was having the Car Club's Vintage Car restoration company do a major overhaul of his vehicle. Sniff had recently closed his cargo transfer terminal after 30 years, which transferred cargo from freight boxcars to semi-trailers. With the decline of railcars to move cargo, the terminal was no longer profitable. Sniff lamented his fear to the overhaul crew that the terminal might be vandalized as it sat unused and empty. Several members of the homelessness committee that worked at Bonneville's restoration company came up with a novel idea.

They knew that people without apartments or homes lived in their cars. Living in a car was bad enough, especially during the brutal winter months. They thought about allowing cars to park in the heated terminal at night. Almost all of drivers would leave in the morning to go to work or take their kids to school. The terminal could easily hold over 250 cars while providing access to bathrooms, showers, and most importantly, safety. With the possibility of up to 750 people per night, Sniff knew they would have to increase the number of bathrooms, build a dozen shower cubicles, and purchase a large commercial water heater. Sniff felt excited about the transformation of his terminal. He agreed to lease it to the committee as long as they paid the utility bill and acknowledged that he would not be held liable for any injuries that occurred in the terminal. Roadmaster thought of having a free sandwich bar that offered a different type of sandwich every day, and with peanut butter and jelly for the kids on Friday nights. What about a mobile laundromat? How about a doctor to do wellness checks, especially for the children?

Marks used $50,000 from his campaign fund to retrofit the terminal for its new purpose.

The Car Club members started looking for people sleeping in their cars, vans, and pickups. They left notices on their windshields about the terminal that read:

Come spend the night in your vehicle where it's safe and warm – FREE!! NE Chouteau Trafficway and Martin Ave. Sniff Terminal.

For the first week of its operation, Marks was at the terminal to greet each driver as they approached the on-ramp of the terminal. The number of cars slowly increased to 100 by the end of the week as the word spread through various social media platforms. After one month, the count swelled to 175.

Marks's terminal project did not resolve the homelessness problem, but at least it improved the health and safety of hundreds of adults and children in his district.

CHAPTER 8: KINGSLEY

Marks's political opponent in the congressional election, John Weldon Kingsley, skipped town the day before his two henchmen attempted to firebomb his opponent's home.

Marks was convinced he would continue to be a target, and that Kingsley would continue seeking his revenge on Marks. Waiting for Kingsley to make his next move was not a good plan. First, he would have to find out where Kingsley went. Listening to the mind of Cloy Probst, one of the henchmen, indicated that Kingsley went to Quebec City, Canada. Marks put his detective agency to work to verify that destination. No airline flight from Kansas City listed Kingsley as a passenger. They expanded their search area to discover that Kingsley had taken a flight from Jefferson City to Chicago then to Quebec City. With its population of over half a million souls, it would take some legwork to find him.

All the field investigators at the detective agency wanted to make the trip to find Kingsley. Bonneville drew two names out of a hat, Studebaker Silverhawk and Hudson Hornet. They decided to take their wives with them and drive the 1,500 hundred miles in the Hornet, combining business with a little pleasure.

The only clue they had about Kingsley was his love of fancy cars. When Silverhawk and Hornet arrived in the city, they visited numerous dealerships that sold expensive cars. They showed a photo of Kingsley, but no one had seen him.

They started researching cars for sale in the current and back issues of newspapers. Only three expensive cars had been sold. They tracked down the sellers to see if Kingsley had been the buyer. No luck. Silverhawk and Hornet decided to see if they could determine where Kingsley was living. They spoke to the doorman of every upscale hotel in the city. No one had seen him. Maybe he was staying with a friend or relative. The phone book was not much help, either.

They called Bonneville for assistance with reaching Kingsley's former secretary; hopefully, she could provide some information about him that might benefit the search. She told them that Kingsley visited Quebec City on a regular basis to go fishing with an old business associate, but she could not recall his name. She remembered he had talked about a boat when they went fishing. Lesson learned: They should have talked with her before coming north.

The following day, the two Car Club members and their wives, all dressed in casual clothes, nonchalantly examined the boats along the St. Lawrence River. Knowing that Kingsley was rich, they guessed his friend was also rich and owned a boat. After visiting several marinas, they met a crew hand, busy scrubbing a yacht, who had seen Kingsley. The crew hand pointed to a 40-foot yacht, the Crazy Eight, at the end of the dock.

A fisherman was aboard the Crazy Eight and informed them that the owner, Bernard Remillard, and two guests were going fishing tomorrow morning. Hornet and Silverhawk left abruptly and returned an hour later with $50 cash for the fisherman and a card for him to give to the owner's guest, John Kingsley.

"Please give the card to Mr. Kingsley as soon as he comes aboard," requested Hornet.

The card said:

Enjoy your fishing trip – it may be your last.

Sincerely,

Congressman and Mrs. Cliff Marks

P.S. Hope we didn't spoil your day.

Early the next morning, Silverhawk and Hornet were watching the yacht with binoculars from several hundred yards away. They saw Kingsley glancing around as he read the card while talking animatedly to the fisherman and waving the card at him.

The crew found Remillard's home then left a Molotov cocktail (but full of water) in the driveway where it could not be missed. The note read:

We had some leftover, boss! — Cloy

They parked across the street from the driveway and waited for the owner's return. As expected, the car stopped halfway up the driveway and the driver got out to inspect the bottle.

"Think it's for you, John?" Remillard angrily yelled.

As he returned to his car, he noticed Silverhawk and Hornet standing next to their Hudson. He walked down the driveway and approached the two men, who met him in the middle of the road.

"I think you've made your point," Remillard told them.

"We're just getting started," Hornet quickly replied. "Your houseguest has tried twice to kill a US congressman. Two of his henchmen were killed in a gunfight with the congressman's bodyguard, and another two are in jail for firebombing the congressman's home. Did he tell you that? You can expect a federal warrant for his arrest within the week. The congressman, Cliff Marks, will call his friend,

Robert Speelman, US District Attorney in Kansas City, tomorrow morning and tell him where to find your houseguest. I'm sure you don't want to be found harboring a criminal."

"Who are you two?" asked Remillard.

"We work for a detective agency in Kansas City. We were hired to find John Weldon Kingsley and keep track of his whereabouts," Silverhawk answered.

"He won't be here tomorrow morning," said Remillard, as he turned and headed back to his car.

About an hour later, a taxi arrived and picked up Kingsley. The Hudson followed it to Quebec City's Jean Lesage International Airport. Kingsley bought a ticket for a flight to New York City. Hornet's wife, Sissy, who Kingsley had never seen, took the same flight while the rest of the crew drove nine hours south to New York City.

The next day, a fruit basket was delivered to Kingsley's room in the Plaza Hotel. The note attached said:

Enjoy your stay in New York City. – Congressman and Mrs. Cliff Marks

Kingsley was so mad that he threw the fruit basket against the wall and stomped on the fruit while screaming profanities at Marks.

Just a few minutes later, the hotel security guard and the assistant manager knocked on his door. After seeing the mess on the wall and floor, they informed him that he was no longer a welcomed guest in the hotel. They asked him to pack his bags and pay the $1,200 bill for his night's stay and cleanup.

The Car Club crew was waiting for him in the lobby, along with two US marshals who had a warrant to arrest Kingsley.

During their drive south, the Car Club crew learned that Cloy Probst had finally turned against Kingsley. Probst secretly recorded the conversation when Kingsley instructed him to firebomb a congressman's home – which happened to be a federal crime.

CHAPTER 9: NOT ENOUGH JUICE?

Marks was sitting in the House chambers when his cell phone beeped and the red encryption light blinked.

"Who's calling?" asked Marks.

"Sir, this is Phil Hillsborough at the Syntil operation center."

"Must be important for you to call me."

"Yes, sir. Jordan Walker is out of the country. Something spooky happened about an hour and a half ago. There have always been electronic monitors on all the implants, just in case the implants might wake up, so to speak. Your wife's monitor alarmed twice this morning. The first time, we thought there might've been a random voltage spike. But the second alarm, which went off about 45 minutes ago, almost made me fall out of my chair. The alarm was for real! Mrs. Marks's implant was operating, but only for 10 seconds. It appears that the implant's software program was starting to boot up."

"After all this time of being inactive, that *is* spooky. What happened?" asked Marks.

"Not sure. Can you tell me what your wife's been doing this morning?" Phil inquired.

"She was home. I called her from my office and asked her to look in my den for my powerpack because I forgot to bring it with me today. I mistakenly thought I would be home by mid-afternoon and would not need any supplemental power for my implant. I sent Jerome to Gleason to get the powerpack. Gloria found it in the den and brought it to the front door to give to Jerome."

"Has she ever handled your powerpack before?"

"No. There's no reason she would've until today," replied Marks.

"I haven't talked to the design engineers, but I think the powerpack provided the energy her implant has always been missing for it to be operational."

"Holy shit! This is going to knock my wife off her feet. Do you have any indication that she might know her implant was trying to boot up?" asked Marks.

"None. The powerpack wasn't close enough to her implant for a long enough time to have any effect on her brain. She doesn't know!" answered Phil.

Phil was trying hard to be cool and professional, but Marks could hear the excitement in his voice.

"I'm sure the design engineers will want to repeat the events of today," said Phil.

"What about the other implants that don't work? I don't want my wife knowing this until Dr. Candle can be consulted and with Gloria when she learns what happened. At the same time, we're making a big assumption that if she were connected to the powerpack, her implant's computers will fully boot up and become operational."

"Yes, sir. It's a huge assumption. Her implant was turned off shortly after it was embedded in her brain because only a couple of her receivers worked, and the word interpreter never worked. She was getting a lot of emotional input, which made it impossible for her to function. It just might've been a lack of energy for the implant to work."

"When you get a chance to speak with the design engineers, let me know how the Deuces project manager and upper management want to proceed. I expect they'll agree to confine this information about Gloria and not give the others with implants any false hope."

"Yes, sir. I'll send classified encrypted emails to all interested parties to report to operations without telling them what has happened. I'm sure there will be a crowd in the control center within the hour, wanting to hear and see what's going on. The operation center hasn't called 'All hands on deck' since your implant went operational. That was an exciting day."

"You were on duty that day?" asked Marks.

"Yes, sir. And I don't mind saying…there were a lot of people with tears in their eyes. You were a long time coming, Mr. Marks. After five disappointments, we were at a low point in the program, and the fear was real that the company was going to give up on the effort. At my level in the company, I didn't know how much money had gone into the program, but based on the number of scientists and engineers, it must be a lot," Phil stated.

"Four hundred million," Marks blurted out before realizing he probably should not have disclosed that information.

"Holy Batman! They bet the ranch on this program."

"They did, so you can understand why the CEO gets a little hostile on occasions. You keep that number to yourself, Phil."

The CEO of Syntil called Marks within the hour on his encrypted phone. Lance Winford was clearly excited.

"Cliff, this is amazing news and a tremendous advancement for the program. I'm truly excited for Gloria! I'll be present with you and Gloria when Dr. Candle can make it to Washington. Have you told Gloria?"

"No! Not a word until Dr. Candle is with Gloria. Have you briefed Dr. Candle?" said Cliff.

"She's in Idaho, but the operation center fully briefed her on a secure link as to what has transpired. I understood your feelings and totally support not telling the other implants until we confirm that Gloria's implant will function. I'll coordinate my travel plans with Candle."

Marks told Gloria that Lance Winford and his wife, Linda, were coming to do some congressional lobbying. They also wanted to review the contract with the detective agency responsible for completing the security clearance of potential Syntil employees. Bonneville Taylor would lead the discussions for a partnership since he knew the detective agency's costs and profits.

Marks had to wait four days before the key players could visit Gleason. Everyone was excited to see if the powerpack would provide the needed electrical energy to fully energize Gloria's implant. Walter Champion, Chairman of the Board of Syntil, would also be in attendance, along with his trophy wife, Heather, 15 years his junior.

Marks and Heather met during the election campaign at a charity event. He learned she did not care much for him. Everything about Marks baffled her. His background as a construction mason and his relationship with the Vintage Car Club, with their gangster aura, seemed nonsensical to her. She wondered how a nobody could have such a beautiful wife, fancy clothes, a penthouse apartment, a big mansion, and have money to throw around at a $5,000-a-plate charity dinner? But most of all, Heather pondered, is how could a novice with absolutely no experience in politics possibly beat a well-connected and shrewd politician, like Kingsley, in the upcoming election? When she made her feeling about Marks known to her husband, his reply startled her.

"We are both voting for Cliff Marks," said Champion.

"Walter, that's absurd!"

"I couldn't be more serious. Our voting for Marks isn't negotiable, Heather! And you'll tell all your snooty, bitchy friends to vote for him. You might think I won't know who you vote for, but I'll know if you don't vote for Marks because one thing you aren't good at is hiding your feelings. Cliff Marks is the smartest person I know. His IQ is off the charts, his knowledge has no limits. He's an honest man who cares about people. He'll serve our city and its people with honesty and dignity, and he'll be a congressman for as long as he wants. Lastly, and more importantly, he knows exactly how *you* feel about him – and he still holds no ill feelings toward you," Champion asserted.

He glanced around the room and spotted Marks. He took Heather's arm and they worked their way through the crowd toward Marks. Heather started to resist, but due to Champion's firm grip on her arm, she came along willingly.

Marks was talking with a handsome black man Heather did not know. She was surprised that he was at the charity ball. His suit looked expensive. She wondered if he was a model or professional athlete.

"Good evening, sir and Mrs. Champion," Marks greeted them. "May I introduce my friend and business partner, Bonneville Taylor? Bonneville, this is Walter Champion, Chairman of the Board of Syntil, and his lovely wife, Heather."

"Pleasure to meet you both," replied Bonneville.

"Mr. Taylor, what do you do for a living to afford that beautiful suit?" Heather inquired. Asking personal, probing questions went hand in hand with her arrogant personality and the feeling of power that wealth brings.

"Glad you like the suit; it's a rental. I came from a background that would consider spending $5,000 on this piece of clothing to be wasteful and foolish, no matter how wealthy one is. I can't take credit for picking it out. Cliff's tailor, Jameson, chose it for me. I didn't want to embarrass my partner by coming in some off-the-rack rag," said Bonneville, smiling.

"I can see your partner doesn't share your thrifty opinion about clothing," responded Heather.

"We run in different crowds," said Bonneville. "My crowd would think I was skimming money from the company."

"What crowd and company is that?" persisted Heather.

Knowing that Bonneville did not like being pushed around and Heather's feelings about the Car Club, Marks injected himself into the crossfire.

"Bonneville is the president of the Vintage Car Club. Some folks think the club is run by a bunch of gangsters…and it was. Bonneville spent five years purging the lawless elements from the Car Club and built it into a profitable vintage car restoration business. The revenue from the business is plowed back into the community. The Car Club members are a key component in my election campaign to get out the vote," said Marks.

Walter Champion chimed in the conversation. He spoke at length about the De Ville Detective Agency's contract with Syntil to do the security clearance on new employees.

"Okay, okay. He's not only handsome, but also a nice guy. My apologies, Mr. Taylor," replied Heather good-naturedly.

Gloria, with a mischievous smile and a drink in hand, joined the group.

"Gloria, Heather was curious as to how I was able to get you to marry me?" Marks stated.

"That's easy…but polite company and social morals often get in the way of fully understanding. However, if we could set them aside, I'm sure Cliff could give you a convincing demonstration," said Gloria, putting her arms around Heather's waist, giving her a little squeeze.

"On second thought, I'll take care of the demonstration," said Gloria, patting Heather on her ass. "Come on, sweetie! Let's dance," she continued, as she handed Cliff her drink and pulled Heather toward the dance floor.

Champion, his wife, and Bonneville were confused by Gloria's comment, except her husband, who knew exactly what his closet bisexual wife was talking about. She was going to pull Heather into her web of sexual pleasure. Gloria knew she was hard to resist, even by a hardcore homophobe.

Marks told Gloria that Dr. Molly Candle, along with her husband, Gordan Tillman, was going to do a psychological evaluation him. She was always looking for changes in his ability, personality, and behavior.

Phil Hillsborough and a software engineer from Syntil were coming to do some tests on Cliff's implant and the backup power battery. All of these were half-truths, so as not to get Gloria's hopes up.

The day the visitors arrived, the Gleason estate's kitchen staff were laying out an impressive lunch. Three servers were carefully putting all the china and flatware in place on the table. Jerome and Margaret Koluccy were tasked to be the greeters. The black SUVs drove into the underground garage, and the guests were brought up the service elevator to the main floor. Marks also directed them to take Gordan Tillman, Bonneville, Linda Winford, and Heather Champion on a tour of the city after lunch. Marks and Gloria stood in front of the large fireplace in the living room to receive their guests.

Dr. Greg Olson was a surprise addition to the group. He quickly apologized for inviting himself, but Marks would hear none of it.

"It's great to see you. I'm embarrassed I didn't call you, doc," said Marks, as he shook the doctor's hand and gave him a hug – two behaviors totally out of character for Cliff Marks.

With a drink in hand, Gloria gave the group a tour of the library, parlor, drawing room, den, foyer, office, recreation room, sunroom, and ended with the dining room.

Marks could tell that the group from Syntil was anxious to do the test on Gloria's implant.

After an enjoyable lunch, five of the guests, Gordan Tillman, Heather Champion, Bonneville Taylor, Margaret Koluccy, and Linda Winford (who were not involved in nor aware of Syntil's confidential Project Deuce implant program), went to their rooms to change into casual clothes for a tour of the city, while everyone else gathered in the den. Phil Hillsborough asked Gloria to help test the battery's strength by holding it at different distances from her husband. He said the engineers wanted to know how far Marks could be from the powerpack and it still provide additional juice to the implant.

The two Syntil executives and two doctors sat quietly in overstuffed chairs, watching as Gloria moved around the room. Sometimes, her body shielded the powerpack from Marks. Hillsborough recorded and called out the signal strength and separation distance from the powerpack. They heard that the powerpack's effectiveness greatly decreased beyond 15 feet, but could still power the implant from 25 feet away.

After approximately 10 minutes of moving around the den, Gloria started getting a strange look on her face. She tilted her head upward, as if trying to listen to a distant sound. She seemed no longer aware of everyone present or anything in the room. She finally stopped following Hillsborough's instructions. He became silent and focused on the data displayed on his laptop computer.

Dr. Candle was the first to break the silence.

"Gloria, what's wrong?" she asked.

"Not sure."

"Are you hearing a lot of voices?"

"Yes," she replied, closing her eyes as she sat down next to Dr. Candle.

"We think the powerpack might be strong enough to activate your long-dormant implant," said Candle.

Gloria jerked her head toward Candle and mouthed a silent 'WHAT?'

"We're all as shocked as you must be. Focus your attention on me. There's probably a lot of noises in your head, so just look at me and think only about me. It takes 20 minutes for the sensors, receivers, transmitters, and the 24 central computer processors to be activated," said Dr. Candle, as she looked at Hillsborough for a progress report on the activation progress of Gloria's implant.

A tear ran down Gloria's cheek. Her face was grimacing as if she was in pain. The powerpack had slipped from her hand onto the floor. Dr. Olson saw it fall. He quickly darted across the room to pick it up then set it on the couch next to Gloria. Dr. Olson looked at Hillsborough and received a thumbs up.

As an experienced ER doctor, Greg Olson could see that Gloria was under stress and did not look well. The small beads of sweat popping up on her forehead worried him, so he took charge.

"Gloria, you need to lie down. Cliff, get some small bags of ice. Molly, get your medical bag, so we can start an IV. Gloria, are you in pain?" Olson asked.

"I'm hot and my body aches all over," Gloria weakly replied.

After a long, silent few minutes later, Hillsborough announced that Gloria's implant was completely activated. By then, Marks had returned with several plastic bags of ice, which Olson placed on Gloria's head. Candle had secured an IV and portal line in Gloria's right arm and slowly injected 150 mcg of Fentanyl into the portal to mitigate her pain.

"Cliff, we need to put Gloria to bed," said Olson.

"I got just the man to do that," said Marks, walking into the foyer and yelling for Jerome.

Jerome and Alexis were standing in the foyer, ushering guests into the elevator to head down to the cars in the basement garage.

After telling Alexis to go ahead and that he would meet them out front, Jerome ran across the foyer toward Marks.

"Gloria's not feeling well. Please carry her up to her bedroom," Marks directed.

Jerome shot Marks a skeptical look until he walked into the den and saw Gloria laying on the couch with her eyes closed. He looked back at Marks, who shrugged his shoulders. Jerome, like Stu Nichols, revered Gloria – for her to be sick was disturbing.

"Watch out for the IV in her arm when you pick her up, Jerome," cautioned Candle.

"Yes, ma'am," Jerome replied while gently slipping his massive arms under Gloria's body, easily lifting her from the couch.

"I've got you, Mrs. G," said Jerome. He followed Marks and the two doctors up to Gloria's bedroom.

Marks and Jerome left Gloria with the doctors and walked downstairs. Marks knew he wanted to know what was wrong with Gloria, but Jerome did not ask.

"She'll be fine by tomorrow morning, Jerome. Have fun giving the ladies a tour of the city," said Marks, escorting Jerome to the front entrance, where the cars were waiting for him.

Marks walked back to the den. The two Syntil executives and Hillsborough were nervously awaiting his return.

"Gentlemen, Gloria's bodily reaction to the implant mirrors what my body went through twice when the implant was turned on. The initial activation of my implant happened after my accident, when I was in a coma, so I didn't feel or remember anything. The second time was when you, Walter, turned my implant off and on. It's not a pleasant feeling. I really thought I was going to die. So, from practical experience, I believe that after the ice packs and some rest, Gloria should recover from the initial shock by morning. She'll probably feel like she has a bad hangover. On the bright side, her implant is activated and functioning properly," reported Marks.

"Great, great news for the program and for Gloria," said Walter Champion. "I want you to know, Cliff, that I caught a lot of shit for turning your implant off and on during our first meeting at company headquarters. Michael Bocelli still loves to jab me in the ass about it. None of us had any idea of the impact. It's one of those mistakes that you carry with you forever. My apologies," said Champion.

"Phil, let everyone back at the control center know that an increase in power was all it took to activate her implant. This is unbelievable! So simple a fix…and to be discovered by chance," said Winford. He raised his hand and continued, "Yes, I know that before we can declare total success, we have a lot of tests to run on the capabilities the implant will give Gloria. Still, this is one hell of a milestone. Cliff, when do you think the testing process can begin?" asked Winford.

"I'll check with Dr. Candle, but I think tomorrow afternoon. Her initial problem will be blocking out what she doesn't want to hear. The fewer people in the room with her, the better. She'll be overwhelmed in a crowd until she learns how to turn off some of her receivers. I'll show her how to do that tonight, so she doesn't have to hide in her room during your visit. Tomorrow, we'll act like everything's fine, like Gloria just has a bad headache. We don't want anyone outside the program to wonder what's going on. Jerome won't say a word to anyone that Gloria had anything more than a headache," said Marks. "Someday in the future, I'll ask your permission to grant him access to the program. I don't like pushing him away by shutting him out of what's happening around him. He's been with me from the beginning with the implant. As they say, he would take a bullet for me and for Gloria."

"Excellent, Cliff," Champion responded. "Lance, you and I can continue with our cover story and go visit some congressional members and senators tomorrow. Cliff, you set up some meetings, right?"

"Yes, sir," said Marks.

"Okay, good. Lance, unless you disagree, I think Cliff can brief Jerome on the program," said Champion.

"I agree. Anyone that's such an integral and important part of Cliff's life should be part of the program," said Winford.

"Thanks," said Cliff. "Can I call the staff to get you a drink?"

The two doctors were successful in reducing Gloria's temperature and relieving her pain, but it took the rest of the afternoon for her body to recover from the shock. Marks taught her how to turn off most of the receivers to reduce the workload on her mind. Gloria wanted to join the group for dinner, but Marks convinced her to wait until breakfast.

Gloria was awake before sunrise, so she decided to go to her office downstairs. She called the night security guard and asked him to find Phil Hillsborough to tell him to come to her office and bring his computer.

Phil knocked on her office door within 10 minutes.

"How can I help you, Mrs. Marks?"

"I want to do the tests on my implant."

"You don't think we should wait for Dr. Candle?"

"No, I'm not going to wait. This is too important to wait. I want our bosses to know that the lack of power was the only thing needed for the implant to work properly. If I don't feel good, we can call Dr. Candle. Come on, let's do this," Gloria insisted.

"I don't want to get in trouble with your husband," said Phil. Gloria could sense that he was uncomfortable and wanted to escape.

Gloria realized that Phil was uneasy about the way her body looked. She had dressed quickly this morning and had only put on sweatpants and a T-shirt, but no bra. Gloria slipped into a blue cardigan that was hanging on the back of her office chair and buttoned it up.

"Sorry about that, Phil. I sometimes forget I've got these big puppies. Think we can start with the first test?" she asked.

"Sure. Let me turn on my computer. Okay, you only have two of your receivers turned on. Do you know what color I'm thinking about?"

"No."

"Okay. Slowly turn on one receiver then another until you know what color I'm thinking about."

When the fifth receiver was activated, Gloria shouted, "Blue puppies! Oops, sorry...but that's what you were thinking."

"True –it's a male thing. Moving on! Now, I'm thinking of a sentence. Tell me what it is."

"Yellow is the color of her hair."

Phil responded, "Excellent! Your implant knows which receiver must be turned on in order to communicate with me, and it will do so automatically from now on. More importantly, we know that your word interrupter is working. So, the implant turns the electrical impulses from your brain into binary code then into words. Let's try the reverse. Use your implant's transmitters to put a number or word in my brain."

"Got it. You put the number five in my brain," said Phil.

"Yes! Now, I'll send you a sentence," she continued.

"'I love pool parties' is the sentence," said Phil.

"Right. What's next?" asked Gloria.

"Let's use your implant to make a phone call. Just think about what you want to do and who you want to call."

"Okay. I'll call you," she agreed.

Phil's cell phone rang a few seconds later.

"Hi, Phil. It's me, Gloria," she said.

"You're doing great, Mrs. Marks. Want to try out your foreign language ability?"

Gloria quickly shuffled through eight different languages and was able to understand them all. She had to verbally repeat each language several times before her mouth and tongue worked properly to pronounce the unique dialects and sounds.

The last test was to access the Internet to obtain information. This took several attempts before Gloria understood which thought process she could use to get the implant to react correctly.

"Well, you passed all the tests. It must be an extremely exciting day for you and the company, and very gratifying to all the engineers and scientists who worked on the project for so many years. We have successful implants with Cliff, Robbie, and now...you. I assume the company will want to see if the implants in Jordan Walker and Marie-Claude Gigot can be activated. A lot of emails are popping up on my computer from the operation center. They've been tracking your tests – and they're pumped, Mrs. Marks!" Phil stated.

Gloria was beaming as she made a grand entrance to the dining room, where everyone was already seated and eating breakfast. The men stood and greeted her. She, along with the implant development engineers, crowded into the operational control center; they were all anxious to see how she and her implant would react in a crowd.

Gloria noticed Phil whispering in Lance Winford's ear, which brought a big smile to Winford's face. *Phil must be telling Lance about the success of the tests he had performed on my implant*, she thought.

Carston appeared at Gloria's side and seated her at the head of the table. Not skipping a beat, Kate O'Rourke came with a plateful of Gloria's favorite breakfast foods.

"Sorry I missed dinner last night. It was fortunate we had two doctors to ease my symptoms. I've never had a headache like that before. It lasted about eight hours then I suddenly started feeling better. I wanted to come down for dinner last night, but Cliff insisted I stay in bed," said Gloria, as she began eating.

She was able to focus on the two people sitting closest to her, Heather Champion and Margaret Koluccy. Earlier,

Marks had arranged their seating place cards to this setup. Marks had learned that both women had clear, focused minds, which would make it easy for Gloria's implant to follow and understand. Most people's minds jump from one topic to another nearly every second, which takes energy and concentration to follow and to try to understand. Marks had been lucky being in a hospital room after his accident, as he dealt with one or two people at any given time. He taught Gloria how to turn her receivers off and on, so she could find the right receiver for the specific person's mind she wanted to listen to. It took Marks time to learn about that option with his own implant. He was not given an operational manual because it did not exist.

When she finished eating, Gloria turned off all her receivers to concentrate on their guests, who were also done with their breakfasts.

"Hey, everybody! I'm not sure what your plans are today, but we're having a pool party all afternoon and a BBQ at 5:00 p.m. It'll give Cliff a chance to show off his muscles. Please let Carston know if you can make it, so the staff will be prepared to feed everyone. At about 8:00 p.m. in the foyer, there will be a dance, complete with a band and singer. Carston, the staff, and their family members are included in the invitation," Gloria announced.

Carston was standing behind Gloria's chair and pulled it out as she stood, which unofficially proclaimed that breakfast was over.

The pool party and BBQ were a huge hit. The dance was attended by well over 50 people, all moving around like their lives depended on it. Marks had the last dance with Heather Champion until the band finally stopped playing. They were the only people left in the spacious room, except for two security guards standing in the dark against the wall.

"I asked Gloria if she was kidding about a demonstration from you about why she married you," Heather whispered in his ear.

"Heather, she was kidding," Marks replied.

"She told me that she wasn't kidding, and that you have the green light for a demonstration."

"Heather, this won't help my political career."

"Open marriages and consenting adults. Come on," Heather insisted.

"Okay, just a demonstration – not full-throttle sex, okay?" said Marks.

At the breakfast table the following morning, Heather took a seat next to Gloria, leaned toward her, and said, "Christ, Gloria. You should've warned me. Cliff is hung like Sea Biscuit!"

Gloria giggled. "Too bad it was only a demonstration. Are your nipples sore?"

"Oh my God. I thought he was going to suck them right off my chest. He wouldn't leave them alone. It's amazing how they could hurt so much, yet feel so good."

"Did you tell him to stop?" asked Gloria.

"Hell, no. I kept sticking my chest out more and saying 'Yes, yes, yes!'"

Heather's admission made Gloria laugh so hard that it became contagious; Heather could not help but join in her laughter. All 12 guests at the table stopped what they were doing to look at the two women and wondered what the joke could be. One server was startled to the point of almost spilling coffee on a guest's hand as she refilled their cup. Both women were blushing and had tears in their eyes as they put their hands over their mouths to muffle their laughter. When they finally stopped laughing, Gloria raised her arm and looked at her guests.

"Sorry, everyone, but this naughty girl knows how to brighten my day by getting to my funny bone."

CHAPTER 10: THE HEIRESS

"Mrs. Marks, my name is Lynn Cramer. I'm your brother's lawyer."

Gloria was suddenly gripped with apprehension. *Why is she calling me?* she wondered.

"I got your phone number from your father just a few moments ago. Following Sal's instruction, you're the first person he wanted me to notify. I'm sorry to tell you that your brother suffered a heart attack last night and died several hours later in the local hospital."

There was a long, heavy silence. Cramer could hear a muffled conversation in the background.

"Ms. Cramer, this is Cliff Marks. My wife can't talk at the moment. Her brother's death is quite a shock to her. She's normally very stoic about death, but with no forewarning of ill health, this one blindsided her. Is there anything else you need to tell her?" Marks asked.

"Yes, sir. Your wife doesn't need to do anything. Sal has documented specific funeral arrangements, which I have been instructed to carry out. Your wife is the sole beneficiary of her brother's estate. If you'll notify Sal and Gloria's parents, I'll come with the trucking company's corporate jet to pick all of you up tomorrow. That is, if your wife agrees. My father has been the lawyer for Sal and the trucking company for many years. Sal had me take over that role when my father retired last year. Please tell your wife that she and her new company are my sole clients, so I'm available to her at any and all times, for both legal and personal matters. My father wasn't only Sal's lawyer, but also his trusted advisor – his consigliere, if you will. I hope I can fulfill those same roles for your wife. If she has any questions, big or small, ask her to call or text me. I'll text her my email address and phone number. I'll make hotel reservations for everyone when she gives me a head count."

It took Gloria several hours before she could call her parents. After that upsetting and tearful conversation, she pulled herself together enough to call Lynn back.

"Ms. Cramer, this is Gloria Marks."

"Thank you for calling. Please accept my condolences for your brother's passing. How can I help you, Mrs. Marks?"

"I'm not sure. I'm embarrassed to admit that I wasn't aware of Sal's bad health," said Gloria.

"He wanted it that way, Mrs. Marks," Cramer replied.

"I suppose. I read the schedule you texted me. It looks good. I was surprised to hear that my brother's company is big enough to have its own jet."

"The company can easily afford the aircraft. It has zero debt, and over the last five years, the annual profit has exceeded $40 million. You're inheriting an excellent business. Sal expressed how he hoped you wouldn't sell it," Cramer paused before continuing. "I'll be coming to pick you up tomorrow morning. We can talk more on the flight."

"How many can come on the jet?"

"Twelve passengers."

"Okay, there will be a total of six, counting myself, three security guards and my parents in Kansas City."

"Your husband isn't coming?" Cramer asked in disbelief.

"Oh, he's coming, but for security reasons, he and six others – his congressional aide, business partner, physician, and three bodyguards – will be coming in a corporate jet. They'll match our schedule," replied Gloria. "He also has to stop in Kansas City to pick up his business partner and physician. He plans on spending some time there on the return trip. By the way, is there a bar on this jet?"

"Since you asked, I'll make sure there is. Looking forward to meeting you, Mrs. Marks. We should arrive at Ronald Reagan Airport at 10:00 a.m. your time tomorrow morning. I'll see you then."

———————————

Lynn Cramer and her office staff did background research on their new boss, who they knew extraordinarily little about. They knew Gloria was the heir, but were caught off guard by Sal's sudden death. They started with the Kansas City newspapers then the Internet. The operations manager at the trucking company called to asked if she had seen the YouTube videos of Mrs. Marks in her one-sided fights. Cramer searched for the footage and quickly found it. She was amazed. She viewed the clips several times to make sure what she had seen was Mrs. Marks. One thing was sure, the macho men at the trucking company would be ill-advised to give their new boss any crap.

Photos of Gloria showed a glamorous woman whose appearance was impeccable. Her clothes, makeup, jewelry, and carriage – all perfect.

Cramer heard a commotion in the outer office. Her prelegal rushed in, laptop in hand, exclaiming, "Look at this! And we thought she was going to be blown away with her newfound wealth. Shit, look where they live!"

It was a photo of Gleason mansion.

"How in God's name can they afford that place? The market value is over $80 million. It's the premiere residence in the DC area. There's obviously a lot we don't know about these two," said the prelegal.

"We're done digging. Thanks, everyone. We're just nibbling around the edges. They're smart, tough, wealthy, and have bodyguards! They don't need any handholding from us. I've got a 4:00 a.m. flight. Clean this place up, in case we have visitors, and go home," Cramer instructed.

Lynn Cramer was even more perplexed with the newfound information about Gloria Marks. With first impressions being so important, she contemplated what to wear and say when she met her new boss in person.

The following morning, while standing in front of her closet, she said, "What the heck?", and decided to wear her $500 black cowboy boots, a black Stetson, black slacks, a black blazer with a white blouse, and small diamond stud earrings.

––––––––––––

"Lynn, we're being instructed not to shut down the engines upon arrival. This will be a grab-and-go mission, so you can save your welcome speech until everyone's on board," the pilot told her. "Our new boss doesn't fool around when she needs security guards."

The Ritter corporate jet was guided next to an idling, black, two-engine jet, with the Syntil logo on the tail, and was surrounded by security. Two large SUVs were parked next to it. Gloria's security guards quickly moved her and their luggage out of the SUVs and into the Ritter jet. With military precision, both jets were moving down the taxiway within two minutes.

In the cupholder next to Gloria's seat was a fresh Jack Daniel's and water on the rocks.

"Thank you, we're going to get along great," Gloria said, as she took a big swallow then raised her glass to Cramer.

"Thanks, boss."

Cramer gave all the passengers ear buds for ease of conversation.

The pilot's voice crackled over the intercom, "Attention, please. Everyone needs to be buckled in their seats. We're next to take off. We should be in Kansas City in about two and a half hours. It looks like smooth weather ahead. We'll refuel there then continue to Westminster, Colorado."

———————————

Gloria was stunned by the size of the Ritter truckyard, which she could see as the jet flew over the company's mile-long parking lot, terminals, loading dock, and maintenance shops, before landing at the nearby airport.

There was a large, shiny new semi with 'Welcome to Ritter County' painted on the side of the trailer. The semi driver, wearing a black Stetson hat and a black armband, was standing on the front bumper. He waved to Gloria as she exited the plane. She waved back.

"Who's that?" Gloria asked Cramer.

"Don Eckley. There was a big debate among the senior managers over how to greet you. They finally settled on one driver…then there was a drawing by all of the drivers to see who got the honor to pay their respects when you arrived."

Gloria headed straight for the semi. The driver jumped down and took off his Stetson. Gloria gave him a big hug, but she was too emotional to speak for a moment.

"Our most sincere condolences, Mrs. Marks, on the passing of Sal. He'll be missed by everyone at the company. My name is Don Eckley. I won the drawing to pay our respects from all the workforce."

"Thank you, Don. Would you drive me to the company?"

"Yes, ma'am. Do you want them to come with us? There's plenty of room in the sleeper," Don asked, as he nodded at the two bodyguards standing behind her.

Cramer had notified the company via email about Gloria's bodyguards, so the employees would not be surprised about their presence.

Gloria sent a silent message to Cliff that she was going to pay the trucking company a visit. She wanted each worker to know she fully embraced them and the business, and that she was taking the reins today.

Gloria reached down and took off her heels. "Alexis, get me my sneakers," she said, as she handed her the heels.

"Don, tell me about the semi-trailer," she continued.

"Well, it's a brand, spankin' new Peterbilt tractor. It's fully automatic with every electronic gadget you can imagine. It has GPS, so headquarters knows where and how fast the tractor is going at all times. It costs about $280 grand with the sleeper. Only the long-haul trips use the sleeper cabs, which is about half of the fleet. Almost all of our trailers are made by Great Dane. There are many different kinds of trailers, so the cost varies," Don explained.

Alexis returned with the sneakers and everyone piled in the tractor. Twenty minutes later, they rolled into the Ritter truckyard and stopped at the operations center. Don ushered them into the control room that was alit from the glow of four large screens displaying fleet information.

The dozen people in the room stood up when they saw Gloria. She used her implant's ability as she shook hands with each person and called them by their first names. That trick was always a showstopper! People looked at each other, wondering how Gloria knew all their names. As she moved to the front of the room, she asked Don to turn on the overhead lights.

"I'm thrilled to be here, albeit a sad day with Sal not being with us. He wanted me to keep the company, which I intend to do, so everyone rest easy," said Gloria, drawing applause from the staff.

"I intend to get fully involved with you and the operations of the company. I'll learn how to drive, haul freight, change tires, and how these monsters are taken care of in our shops. I'll learn about all the bells and whistles in the control center, too. And just as important, I intended on spending time with our customers, where I think I can contribute the most to the company. They're our life blood. I won't be here all the time because you don't need me all the time. My cell phone will be posted on our internal bulletin board. The company lawyer told me the company is profitable and in great financial shape and has an excellent reputation – thanks to your hard work," Gloria said, while sweeping her arm across the room before applauding them.

She continued, "I'll have a complete audit done on every aspect of the company to get a baseline of our status, so I'll know whether we improve or worsen under my leadership. Please be open and candid with the auditors – they won't be giving out grades. I'll meet with union stewards after the audit is completed, which I'm told for a company this size, will take four weeks. Also, thank you for sending Don Eckley to greet me. I felt that he brought Sal's spirit with him." She moved to the back of the operations center. "Don't feel obligated to come to the funeral. Per Sal's instruction, the graveside ceremony will be very brief."

Chip Terril, the operations manager, stood up. "Mrs. Marks, welcome to Ritter. Sal talked about you all the time and he dearly loved you. Tomorrow, a large group of Ritter people will be at the cemetery. Sal was one of us…and we want to show the community that he'll be missed. Don will drive a flatbed trailer to carry Sal's casket from the funeral home to the cemetery. Cars for Sal's parents, you, your husband, and friends will follow Don. Four more flatbed trailers with side rails will be in the procession and will be full of Ritter people."

It was raining the next morning. People were surprised when Gloria and Cliff decided to ride in the flatbed trailer loaded with the Ritter truckyard staff. Gloria knew how to bond with her employees – and they loved her for riding with them in the rain.

After the ceremony, everyone returned to the massive Ritter warehouse for a social luncheon organized by the company. A small western band was playing in one corner of the building, next to the open bar, both of which helped to raise the mood. Large heaters were set up to ward off the suddenly cool weather and to dry out their damp clothes. Gloria and Cliff stayed, as did her parents, until the band quit playing and last person went home.

Lynn Cramer met with Gloria, Cliff, and her parents in Sal's office to explain Sal's trust.

Gloria was the sole inheritor of the Ritter Trucking Company, as well as Sal's home, cars, and pickup, and several pieces of property scattered throughout the region. She was also the beneficiary of a $2 million life insurance policy, and CDs, cash, and gold coins totaling over $14 million. Sal's parents were each given $2 million from separate life insurance policies. There they all stood, stunned by Sal's wealth.

Lynn Cramer interrupted the family's collective shocked silence. "I can see you all are a bit taken aback by the size of the estate. Sal planned for the future and wasn't a big spender. He took great pride in being able to pass his good fortune on to you. We won't know the full value of the company until the audit is finished, but I'd guess it's in the neighborhood of $850 million."

Gloria let out an exalted whistle at the value of her company and asked, "Dad, did you know?"

"I had a good idea. Your mother and I came out every year, so I could go deer hunting with Sal on one of his properties. I saw the company grow bigger each year. His equipment got better and the yard kept growing. By the way, the property we hunted on must be worth a small fortune in itself. You agree, Ms. Cramer?" George Ritter inquired.

"Absolutely. Gloria, you and Cliff should take the time to see it and think about how you want to protect it. I suggested to Sal that he build a house for a land manager to live in to protect the property from timber and game poachers, and land grabbers. Food for thought," replied Cramer.

The next morning, George Ritter directed Lynn Cramer and the 13 people who had traveled to Colorado to pile into a small bus. They drove for two hours, way up into the mountains, where he had gone hunting with his son. Gloria was amazed at the property's size and agreed with Cramer that the land needed to be protected. Gloria asked her father if he would consider moving to Colorado and managing the land. He quickly accepted her offer. He stayed in Colorado for several weeks for the land survey to begin the process of selecting a site for a home.

Marks and the six others who rode to Colorado in the Syntil jet headed home two days later. Three security guards, her parents, and Gloria stayed in Colorado. She wanted to start her new role as the owner/operator of the Ritter Trucking Company. Don Eckley started giving her driving lessons. True to her word, Gloria visited a different customer every day before flying back to Gleason.

CHAPTER 11: MAKING A BABY

On her way from the trucking company to Washington DC, Gloria stopped in Kansas City. She did this for several reasons: she needed to talk to Margaret Koluccy and Stu, and then bring them, her parents, and Bonneville Taylor to attend the president's fundraiser at Gleason.

Gloria and Margaret met for a two-martini lunch to discuss Margaret's desire to have a baby with Stu. After the second martini, the conversation became more candid.

"Look, I know it seems a little loopy for me to want Stu when you look at our completely different social, educational, and economic backgrounds. I get it… but in my eyes, he's the best-looking son of a bitch I've ever seen, and I want his genes in my babies. My nipples get hard, and I get wet between my legs every time I get near him. No other man has ever caused me to react that way. I've tried everything to get him in bed, but failed at every attempt like a clumsy schoolgirl whose mouth and brain are in two different worlds. I get absolutely silly around him. I saw my face in the mirror one time when I was with him – my eyes looked as if I had just seen a god. Stu might've thought I was on drugs. I considered dosing him with the date rape drug, but that wouldn't work because his whole body would be limp. I lost 15 pounds by going to a personal trainer to get my body in shape. I get looks from other men, so I know my hardware isn't the problem. Gloria, I've done everything except beg. Tell him we don't have to get married…maybe that'll take the pressure off him," Koluccy begged.

"Not to worry. I guarantee that between Cliff and me, we'll get you all the Stu genes you want. I'm meeting with him this afternoon. I'll keep you posted as to when I can get you two together."

After lunch with Koluccy, Gloria headed across town to meet with Stu. She called him that morning to inform him that she was coming to the gym, which surprised and thrilled Stu. He carefully inspected the gym to ensure all the equipment was in its proper place and looked professional. He had jumped at Marks's offer to be the full-time manager of his gym. Stu did not want Gloria, of all people, to think that his transition from masonry work to managing the gym was beyond his ability.

Stu became giddy when Gloria turned on her seductive powers. She looked into his mind and knew his every thought. If Stu was a god in Margaret's eyes, then Gloria was a goddess in Stu's eyes. She told him about her meeting with Margaret and her determination to have his baby. While speaking, she noticed that Stu kept eyeing a large male weightlifter who was working out. Gloria knew what he was thinking.

"Stu, why are you reluctant to go out with Margaret? She's a good-looking woman who could have her pick of the men, but not you. Can you tell me why? Be totally honest. I've seen the DVD of you and Cliff."

"Why the hell did he do that?" Stu asked, tightening his jaw and shaking his head in disbelief.

"There are no secrets between Cliff and me. We know every aspect of each other's lives. Let me ask, do you think about Cliff while lying in bed at night?"

"Yes! He's burned into my brain and I can't get past it. I dream about him all the time. Can you believe I miss him so much that I cry?" Stu's voice cracked with emotion and he had to stop for a minute.

He continued, "I've tried to be around other men, but it doesn't work because I'm afraid to make the first move. Perhaps there's something about me that stops other men from coming on to me...unapproachable maybe. I was never good at being open and talkative, knowing which words to say and not say. Realizing that I liked men as much as women came as a shock to me. I'm still getting used to it. Maybe Cliff was an exception, but I won't know until I'm with another man."

"Stu, I'm looking for ways to make a deal with you. I'll do you a favor, so you'll agree to go to bed with Margaret."

"The favor I want is to be with Cliff."

"If he weren't a congressman, we could agree to a long-term, three-way relationship...sort of polygamy in reverse. But not now. It's not going to happen. There are too many people who have ruined their reputations, careers, and fortunes because they wouldn't control their miscreant sexual behavior. When you're together, it quickly becomes apparent you're more than friends. You and Cliff aren't part of the equation. You two body worshippers had a drunken fling that opened the door for you to enjoy each other's bodies, on which you had worked so hard together. You would never even consider opening that door if you were sober. I understand you wanting to experience the thrill of those emotions again, but they'll just have to reside in your memories."

"If I do agree to a deal, I'm afraid I'll feel obligated to marry her."

"She won't marry you because she'll know you haven't taken her into your heart. Why do you keep looking at the big man doing squats? Have you dreamed about him?" Gloria asked.

"I did last night."

"A good dream?"

"A wet dream."

"Wow! Who else do you dream of?"

Stu hesitated before looking Gloria in the eye. "You. You're the most beautiful woman I've ever seen. I wake up in a cold sweat with Cliff chasing me."

Gloria laughed and said, "Would I replace Cliff in your dreams if I were part of the deal or just give you feelings of remorse for having sex with your best friend's wife? But if having me would clinch a deal for Margaret, I would do it for two reasons. First, we believe that without Margaret's leadership, Cliff wouldn't have been elected, so we owe her big time. Second, I agree with Margaret that you're a handsome and delicious hunk of man. Did you know that? Still, that wouldn't solve your questioning about liking other men besides Cliff." She paused, nodded toward the muscular weightlifter, and continued, "What about I get you a date with that man over there? Would we have a deal then?"

"Could you do that?" Stu asked.

"Yes."

"I'm not sure," he hesitated.

"What attracts you to him? It's Sergio, right?" Gloria inquired.

"Yeah. Notice his slender waist that shows off his chest and hips. I like your slender waist. I won't tell anybody, but for some twisted reason, it makes me horny. I could watch him all day," said Stu.

"If I got you a date, would we have a deal?" asked Gloria.

"Yes."

"Come on, introduce me to him."

"Hell, if I do that, he won't even look at me."

"Better to find out now than later what his preference is – me or thee," smiled Gloria, as they walked into the gym area.

"Hey, Sergio! You're looking good. My boss's wife, Gloria, wanted to introduce herself and thank you for your membership."

Gloria extended her hand. "Nice to meet you. Is there anything we need to add to the gym to give you a better workout?" she asked.

"No, ma'am. Stu's done a great job with his selection of equipment."

Sergio hardly took his eyes off Stu. Gloria did not need her implant to determine Sergio's preference.

"Sergio, I'd like Stu to take you out for a complimentary dinner and drinks. It's my way of thanking you for your patronage," said Gloria.

"Thanks, Mrs. Marks," Sergio replied looking at Stu. "Are you going to take me to one of those cheap bars you go to?"

"No, no, no. He's taking you wherever you want to go, Sergio," Gloria interjected.

"Great. Stu, let me take a shower and we can go. I'm hungry. Nice meeting you, Mrs. Marks," Sergio said before heading to the locker room.

"You notice he hardly looked at me and didn't even ask me to come along? Take him to your apartment after dinner. I know you'll have a memorable night," she suggested.

"Hopefully, you'll still be able to fly with us tomorrow afternoon. Margaret is flying with us, so you can tell her you're all in for making a baby. You're both staying in the big house. I'll make sure your sleeping accommodations are conveniently located."

"Damn, woman. I haven't even said 'Yes' yet!" Stu exclaimed.

"Sergio will make it all come true," said Gloria.

And he did.

On the flight to DC the following day, Stu grinned from ear to ear while sitting next to Margaret. The smile on her face told the whole story.

As soon as Gloria and her Kansas City guests returned to Gleason, she told Cliff about her conversations with Stu and Margaret, and about the surprisingly successful agreement.

"Way to go, wife!" Marks exclaimed, giving Gloria a high five. "Stu didn't stand a chance against your seductive powers and your implant. You know he idolizes you. And you were right about taking marriage out of the equation – Alexis will be happy to know she has a better chance of capturing Stu's attention, and that men are now her main competition. By the way, where are they?"

"I don't know. I'm just going to stay out of the way, so I don't do anything that might jinx the deal," said Gloria.

After being shown their adjoining suites on the fourth floor, Margaret and Stu headed for the pool, beach towels in hand. She wore a skimpy red bikini, and he wore black swimming briefs. Gloria's parents enjoyed drinks on the sun-filled patio. Before joining everyone outside, Bonneville spent an hour with Marks, reviewing a stack of client folders and deciding which ones needed their involvement.

Stu shuffled in late to breakfast the next morning. He and Marks had planned on visiting local gyms to get new ideas for his gym in Kansas City.

"Sorry I'm late. I couldn't get away from Margaret. She drained every sperm cell out of my body. I was halfway out the door and she yelled, 'Where do you think you're going? Get back here. We're not through! This one's for fun.' Having been with her, I don't know what I see in men. My groin hurts, I've got claw marks on my back, and my tongue is raw," Stu said through a wide smile.

"I think you were looking to relive the fun we had," said Marks.

"You may be right. Gloria said that now Alexis will be coming after my body. And that Gloria and Margaret thought I was a delicious hunk. That's probably going to go to my head since Gloria said it. Damn, Cliff. You married a hell of a woman!"

During their drive to the newest gym, Marks asked Stu about his date with Sergio.

"It was okay. We had a great dinner. Sergio had about a dozen drinks. We went to his apartment after and he took me to bed with him. I didn't know what to expect, but he really only wanted a warm body next to him in bed. I didn't know that a man could kiss like him. His kisses were getting my body revved up, but nothing happened because he fell asleep. I'll make sure he doesn't drink as much next time."

CHAPTER 12: MILITARY BUDGET

The week before, Marks had called Lance Winford to confirm that Syntil did not do any business with the United States military.

"Sir, I've decided to use the debate on the military budget in the House next month to increase my presence in the House. We'll learn how much information the implant can record and spit out on-demand. I wanted to make sure I wasn't stepping on any Syntil contracts with the military," said Marks.

"The company has avoided military contracts. They have too many different military organizations, regulations, documentation, and specifications to understand. The learning curve was high, so we either had to do a lot of military contracts or none. We chose none," Winford replied.

"Can I help you?" the receptionist stationed in the Speaker of the House's outer office asked. There were six other people waiting; Marks could tell they had been there for over an hour. Marks had come to see the man whose ribs Gloria had broken in a bar fight two months earlier.

"I'm Cliff Marks. I'd like to speak with Gordan McKinney."

"Marks?"

"Yes."

"Please have a sit and I'll see when he'll be available."

"Sir, a Cliff Marks wants to see you," the receptionist said into her phone.

"Oh, shit. Does he look mad?"

"No."

"Okay, I'll come out in a few minutes," said McKinney.

When McKinney entered the outer office, Marks stood up, extended his hand, and said, "I'm Cliff Marks."

"Good to meet you, sir. How's your wife?"

"Her bone bruise is almost healed. How are you?"

"Still tender, but doing fine."

"Good to hear. You got a few minutes?" asked Marks.

During this brief conversation, McKinney was relieved when he realized Marks had not come to seek revenge on him for grabbing Gloria.

"Sure, come into my office," said McKinney, ushering Marks into his office.

"Have a seat. The coffee is still fresh. Can I get you a cup?" asked McKinney.

"Black is fine," said Marks.

"How can I help you?"

"I need a favor next week when the military budget is on the House floor for debate."

"What can I do?" asked McKinney.

"Get the Speaker to recognize me."

"What are you going to do?"

Marks handed McKinney a written list of his objectives.

It took McKinney several minutes to read and understand the implications. He stated, "Some of this is hard to believe, Cliff, but I think I can convince the Speaker to give you enough time for your plan to unfold in the House. I take it that you have several objectives. You'll want to convince the budget committee that someone's watching them and actually reads and understands the entire budget. Secondly, you'll continue asking questions and drawing attention to areas of cost overrun and program delays if the supporters of the budget won't back your American Homelessness Bill. Thirdly, there's enough slop in the military budget to fund your homelessness program. Have I summarized your objective correctly?" asked McKinney.

"You have," Marks responded.

"You'll make a name for yourself with this display of brainpower, and you'll make a lot of enemies for getting into their cookie jar. You realize that no one will believe you can actually memorize and discuss the entire military budget."

"I understand, but I'll demonstrate I've memorized and can discuss the entire budget, page by page, paragraph by paragraph, and sentence by sentence. I just need someone to challenge me. Would you be interested in setting someone up to challenge me?"

"How could they do that?"

"Pick a random page and ask me what it contains."

"You can do that?" asked McKinney.

"Yes, every time and on any page. I won't even have the budget on my desk."

"Damn, that'll be something to see."

"One more thing, invite your favorite reporter to be in the House gallery."

"You really plan on making a big splash," McKinney said.

"I'm hoping I'll get an invitation to some news programs and interviews with reporters, so I can pitch the American Homelessness Bill. The military budget is simply a vehicle to get me there," said Marks.

"You came at the right time. For your information only, the Speaker of the House thinks the chairman of the finance committee is getting too big for his britches. I'll talk with the Speaker and let you know tomorrow."

After a week-long recess, the House was back in session. The military budget was called to the floor and the debate ensued. Several minutes passed until the House Speaker entered the chamber and replaced his delegate. Marks waited a few minutes then stood to ask to be recognized.

"The gentleman from Missouri, Mr. Marks, is recognized," said the Speaker of the House.

Numerous members of the House turned to face Marks; some did not yet know who he was.

"Thank you, Mr. Speaker. I took the opportunity during the recess to read and commit to memory the military budget. I found $62 billion allocated for the upkeep and maintenance of military property that hasn't been used for years. The majority of the properties have bare ground and growing weeds. Those with buildings are dilapidated and vandalized. According to a nearby property owner, they haven't seen any activity on the properties for years. My guess is this $62 billion is being pigeonholed for use on other projects that may have cost overruns."

"Mr. Speaker, will the gentlemen from Missouri yield?" asked the chairman of the budget committee.

"I will only yield for one question," replied Marks.

"Why has the congressman waited until now to question this allocation?"

"I didn't, Mr. Chairman. I wrote a letter to your committee two weeks ago. When I didn't receive a reply, I went to the committee's chief of staff to inquire. Since he knew I was a junior congressman with no juice, I was told in no uncertain terms that my only relationship to the budget was to either vote 'Yes' or 'No'. My letter pointed out an arithmetical mistake of $287 million on one of the pages. More importantly, I believe numerous military contractors are playing us to increase the cost of their programs. They know that very few military contracts are cancelled. After the original contracts are signed, they later come up with new and highly desirable improvements to the equipment. In almost all cases, the contractor was aware of the improvements, but didn't include them in the original design, for fear the program cost would be too high and they wouldn't be awarded the contract. The contractor dangles the new capabilities in front of the operating commands, who in turn, presses the program manager. The military lobbyists go into a full court press to get their congressional representatives to convince Congress to allocate more money. The programs are delayed while the equipment is redesigned; after that, the factories will require retooling in order to make the design."

"Mr. Speaker, this is ridiculous. No one can commit the entire budget to memory," the chairman interrupted, just as Marks hoped he would.

"Test me if you're doubtful."

"Alright, page 91," the chairman agreed, as he turned to the specific page.

"The first paragraph deals with the cost of new uniforms for the Marine Corps. The cost is $1.8 million," Marks stated, with zero hesitation.

The chairman called out a number of pages, to which Marks quickly replied.

"He must have a hearing aid. Someone's probably telling him what's on each page," asserted the frustrated chairman.

"There's a doctor in the chamber. He's welcome to examine my head, ears, and body to see if I have a hidden hearing device…which I don't."

"Your word is sufficient, Mr. Marks," said the Speaker.

"One final point, Mr. Speaker. There's plenty of loose money in the military budget to fund many smaller, important programs. My American Homelessness Bill is a perfect example. I'll continue to chip away at any budget that has a free ride through Congress and that takes too much from our national treasury. Thank you, Mr. Speaker," Marks stated before taking his seat.

The national and local newspapers covered the story about a young congressman who had taken on the military budget committee chairman with a phenomenal display of brainpower, previously only done by computers. As a result of the comments by Congressman Marks, the debate on the budget was suspended. He served notice that he was on a hunt for money in any budget to fund his homelessness bill. It appears that he has the ability to repeat his tour de force examination of any federal budget that is beyond the ability of the congressional body to read and fully understand.

CHAPTER 13: LOBBYIST

Gloria and Cliff started coming to the Riverside Café during his second term in the House. They met there on Thursday evenings, when most of the congressional members returned to their districts for the long weekend.

Gloria was not in the café when Cliff arrived. He received a text message from Gloria that she was on her way. He took a seat at their usual table in the middle of the dining room. His two bodyguards sat in a booth to the side. When a tall man dressed in an expensive three-piece suit approached Cliff's table, both bodyguards stood up and stepped closer. The stranger noticed their movements; he raised his hands and looked at the guards.

"Just want to talk to your boss, fellas," he said, pulling back the wings of his suit coat to reveal he was not carrying a concealed weapon.

"Have a seat. What can I do for you?" Marks asked, as his guards returned to their booth.

"I represent some people who are concerned about your recent involvement with the defense budget," the stranger answered. He did not introduce himself. Not that it mattered – Marks knew who he was in an instant.

Marks rose from his chair when he saw Gloria and her two bodyguards enter the café. He silently started passing information to her when she arrived at the table. He made a fuss of greeting her with a hug and kiss and then seating her at the table. He needed this time to pass all the information about the stranger to Gloria.

The stranger stood as Gloria walked toward the table. He started to speak, but Gloria raised her hand, immediately silencing him.

She turned to face the bar and positioned her fingers in her mouth to give a shrill whistle. Gloria stopped short when she spotted the waiter darting across the room with a drink in his hand.

"Good evening, Mrs. Marks," he said, placing her drink on the table.

She drained half of her double Jack Daniel's and water before speaking.

"Thank you, Seth. Let's see. I think Mr. Broaderick drinks single barrel scotch, neat," said Gloria, turning toward the stranger.

"Ahh, yes. Thanks," Broaderick replied, clearly confused about how she knew his name and his habits.

"Seth, we'll order as soon as Mr. Broaderick gets his drink. I'm starving," Gloria said, smiling at Seth.

"Yes ma'am," Seth replied before scurrying off to the bar.

"Scott, you've come a long way from a cattle ranch in Montana to being a hotshot lobbyist. Your dad sent you east to get a good education at Yale and you never went back to Montana. You married the daughter of a rich developer and started your own public relations firm. Your reported net worth is $10 million, but my husband knows you have over $30 million in unreported income stashed overseas."

Broaderick started to get out of his chair to protest, but Gloria silenced him.

"Sit down. I'm not through," she demanded and waited for Broaderick to sit.

Gloria continued, "We're impressed that a big-time lobbyist like yourself would waste his time on small potatoes like us. After all, my husband is a junior congressman, and I'm sure the old, long-term, entrenched members of the House aren't going to let him play in their pea patch. You can tell your clients that my husband was just having fun pulling their chains. He wanted to let them know someone's watching, and that someone can actually read and understand the damn thing."

"May I?" he asked.

Gloria nodded.

"Mrs. Marks, I don't think we've met before, yet you seem to know a lot about me. Why is that?" Broaderick queried.

"The congressman and I enjoy reading the hundreds of dossiers that his detective agency has put together on each lobbyist in the Capitol. Of course, he has memorized them all. I just read the heavy hitters, like yours. You have some enormously powerful clients," said Gloria.

"My clients were impressed that Congressman Marks had memorized the complete document. From their standpoint, that was the scary part because he has overcome the two major impediments, or safety fence, if you will, from interference: their massive size and complexity. The congressman has torn a gaping hole in that fence. Your husband spotted $62 billion of wasted money that they'll be forced to remove from the budget. That's not pocket change. Some of that money came out of my clients' pockets. Secondly, there's always a lot of sharks circling the defense budget, searching for ways to take a bite and get some money. Your husband's shown that he's the man who can help them. That situation is the most troublesome because $62 billion may only be the beginning," said Broaderick.

"Gloria, our guest is recording this conversation and his associate is at the far table in the back corner with her camera rolling. Let's all wave to the camera," said Marks, as he and Gloria turned to face the camera, both waving and laughing.

Broaderick bowed his head and covered his eyes with his hand. He knew he was outgunned.

Marks spoke. "I guess Scott's plan was to get me to say something stupid, so his clients would have leverage on me. But then, dear wife, you came along and spoiled everything by letting him know that we know more about him than he'd want to share with the public. You have to realize, Scott, that we know every person you've screwed over and cheated. Trying to pressure us isn't such a good idea. Now that we have that business out of the way, you can invite your associate, Gina Fisher, to join us."

Broaderick reluctantly turned and beckoned to Fisher to come over.

Marks stood up as the short, stocky woman in her late-20s, with glasses and long, thick, black hair, approached their table. Marks pulled out a chair for her.

"Can I get you a beer, Gina?" Marks asked.

"Please," she said, giving him a quizzical look over the top of her glasses.

Gloria waved at Seth, who rushed over to take her order.

"Seth, I think the lady would like a tall Bud Light draft," said Gloria.

"I think we can order now," said Marks. "My wife will have a 12-ounce New York strip, medium-well, with a baked potato, green beans, and a big glass of red wine. I'll take the same, but with a house salad and no wine. What about you, Gina? I'm buying, so order what you'd like."

Gina looked at Broaderick, who shrugged his shoulders and threw up his hands in surrender. "Sure, go ahead. I'll have another drink, Seth," he acquiesced.

"Come on, Scott! It's not often that your target buys you dinner," Gloria said, reaching to give Scott a friendly punch on the shoulder.

Gina looked long and hard at Gloria then at her boss. She asked, "Scott, have you seen the videos of Mrs. Marks in fights?"

"What are you talking about?"

Gina retrieved her phone from her purse. After a few clicks, she handed her phone to her boss. It was a video of Gloria's bar fight.

"Holy shit! That was you?" Broaderick asked Gloria.

She nodded.

"I heard the gossip about the Speaker's chief of staff getting his ass kicked, but I figured it was another bar story blown out of proportion, so I never watched any of the footage. Mrs. Marks, you made it look easy," he complimented.

"It was. Men always underestimate women," Gloria quickly replied. "Just like you underestimated my husband and me. You need to do your homework before you take on new targets."

The first part of dinner was quiet, as they were all famished and excited to eat.

After several minutes, Broaderick broke the symphony of silverware clinking on plates by saying, "Congressman Marks, when people finally realize the implications of what you've done with the defense budget, there'll be a lot of people who'd like you to go away. Re-election is in six months. They're going to throw a lot of money to see that you don't get re-elected. If that doesn't work, they'll take a harder approach."

"They'll have to get in line. I have all sorts of enemies. The four bodyguards over there are part of about a dozen who keep Gloria and me safe. The bad guys are batting zero for five. They tried to harm us on the high seas, in our car, in airports, in our home, and on the campaign trail. And they've failed every time," Marks paused, his tone changing to seem more upbeat. He continued, "I'm unopposed in the upcoming election, so they can save their money and spend it on hitmen. Let your clients know that our bodyguards are not a bunch of old, fat, retired cops. They're all ex-military combat soldiers; they know how to kill and they love a good fight. Gloria and I aren't looking over our shoulders," stated Marks, who happened to stand up the same time as Gloria.

Marks declared, "There are three things you need to do if you want to stay out of trouble. First off, hire a tax lawyer and bring the $30 million back home. Second, put your fishing pole away," he said while shooting Gina Fisher a look. He continued, "And lastly, refund the 50 grand of overbilling you did on your last two clients. If you do those three things, we'll forget you tried setting us up."

Marks turned away from the table and began walking toward the front door.

"Thanks for an entertaining evening," said Gloria, dropping her napkin on the table. She followed her husband as they left the café, their procession led by one bodyguard; the other three trailed behind Gloria and Cliff.

As soon as the Markses were out of hearing range, Gina was on her feet. Her face flushed as she pointed a stubby finger at Broaderick.

"You lying, cheating, cheap bastard! Thirty million? And you pay me slave wages! If you want me to continue being a loyal employee, there better be a very substantial bonus in my checking account tomorrow," Gina demanded in a hushed, angry voice. She threw her napkin at Broaderick and stormed out of the café.

CHAPTER 14: STREET FIGHTER

After Gloria's first street fight at the airport, Marks had asked her if she had always been aggressive and looked forward to a fight.

"Lord no!" was her reply. "I noticed the change in my personality after the diving accident. The brain concussion must've rearranged some of my brain cells. It also brought my bisexuality into my conscious thoughts, which I guess, has always been pulling at me. Those new thoughts and aggressions were spinning around in my head. I drink to push the conflicting thoughts into the background because this body of mine can be a curse. I'm not bragging, but men and women hit on me all the time. Not giving in at times was stressful because I'd get sexually aroused, but have no kind of relief. I just wanted a warm body next to me. Sometimes, while lying in bed at night, I'd pour lotion on my body and move my hands all over, wanting them to belong to someone else. I didn't let sexual pressure make me downplay my body with shoddy clothes, dirty hair, and cheap makeup. I spent a lot of time and money making sure my clothes, hair, and makeup were prefect. In fact, I did everything I could to make my body even more desirable. I swam and worked out with a trainer to keep it in peak condition. I try not to flaunt it, but I guess that maybe I do sometimes."

"Do those thoughts still bother you?" Cliff asked.

"I still have dark thoughts about the swim team raping me and the raw sexual desire and pleasure they released. It scared the hell out of me. I wanted to believe it was just an aberration, but it wasn't – that was the real Gloria. They somehow knew me better than I did because they were gay or bisexual; they knew how to bring my emotions out in the open. I went crazy when my long-hidden sexuality was exposed. I'd never felt that way before. I still get goosebumps all over my body when I think about that night by the pool. I often feel disgusted by the whole affair; other times, I'm disgusted by the unbelievable thrilling sensation of newly discovered enjoyment that I deprived myself of for years. I've relived that night over and over, sometimes with pleasure, and sometimes…not so much. I quit the swim team. I never went back because I was afraid I'd go beyond bisexual and become openly gay. At the time, I believed that I couldn't do that to my folks, but I was wrong. Amazingly, those inner demons took a long vacation when I first met you. You cleared my mind like no one ever has. I feel comfortable and at ease around you, Cliff. You cannot imagine the value of feeling at ease when most of the time, my mind is a whirlpool of unsettling emotions. The first day I walked into your room at the hospital, my mind suddenly cleared, and I was totally focused on you. It was fun interacting with you and the doctors. I'll carry the memories of that wonderful day with me forever."

"Do you like to fight?"

"Yes, the adrenaline rush is amazing! I can appreciate how combat soldiers miss the rush they get from a firefight. The feeling that results is like no other."

"Better than sex?" asked Cliff.

"Yeah, a climax is great, and people do some stupid, nasty things to get the feeling of a sexual climax, but there's normally no immediate danger, like a fight, to heighten the feeling. And it's different than winning a competition. I guess risk and rush come together to create that feeling. I do miss it and look forward to the next fight, even though I might get hurt or killed. For some strange reason, the threat of danger or death is pushed aside. I experience some of that feeling when working with my trainer. He pushes me hard and fast while he increases the intensity of the face-to-face confrontation. He pulls his punches at the last second. I never know if he's going to hit me hard or take it 'easy' on me. He gives me some hard whacks, so I know what getting hit feels like and to learn how to keep focused on the fight and not the pain. He has the obvious advantage due to his skills, but I challenge him because I'm quick at dodging some of his moves. He's actually structured the training around my speed. Quick in-and-out strike tactics, so I stay out of my opponent's reach. We work on dodging, ducking, and weaving away from kicks and punches. You saw in the airport attack where I used my three-inch heels," said Gloria.

"Have you talked about carrying a weapon?"

"Yeah, several times…but I think the shoes are the most inconspicuous. And they're legal in every state. There are very few times when I'm not wearing heels. When that happens, I can use an expandable steel baton, which fits in my shoulder bag," she explained.

"Have you trained with the baton? How quickly can you retrieve it?" questioned Marks.

"Yeah, we found a way to Velcro it to the bottom of my shoulder bag. It takes a second for me to reach down and grab it. I just flick my wrist and the baton extends to 16 inches. You don't want to get hit with a steel baton. I practice getting the baton off the shoulder bag and into my hand, and then striking a big punching bag. I hit the bag so hard the other day, it tore the cover material," Gloria said.

A mischievous smile formed across her face. She continued, "And yes, I bought them a new bag."

Gloria's training and baton came into play one evening, as she and Cliff left their favorite café. Shortly after dusk, the couple journeyed down the sidewalk to their car, which was parked at the next block. Their ever-vigilant bodyguard, Alexis, followed the Markses to ensure their safety. Gloria, Cliff, and Alexis spotted Chad standing by their car. A large van zipped past them and came to a stop several cars ahead; three men jumped out and positioned themselves on the sidewalk between the Markses and

Chad. Alexis immediately moved in front of the Markses. Gloria moved behind her husband and put her back to his, so she would be facing any attack from behind Cliff. Chad saw the men; he whispered into his radio's wrist microphone, "Alexis, I'm coming up on your left flank." He popped the trunk of the car and withdrew a 12-gauge pump action shotgun. He ran down the street until he was lateral to the three men. As soon as Chad stopped, he injected a shotgun shell into the gun's receiver. Everyone heard the unique, distinctive metallic sound of the shotgun's pump action mechanism. Nobody moved.

"Your move, Christoff," Marks coolly stated.

Christoff was confused. He wondered how Marks knew who he was.

Christoff nodded his head, the signal for the fourth man, the driver of the van, to approach the Markses from behind. Gloria noticed him, reached her left arm across her body, and pulled the baton from under her shoulder bag. As her left arm swung forward in a wide arc, she flicked her wrist to extend the baton, landing it directly on the attacker's right forearm. He never saw the baton coming.

Gloria wasn't finished. She quickly switched the baton to her right hand, and with another backswing, struck the man's left wrist. Bystanders could hear his wrist bones crack. The momentum of the attack propelled him forward. Gloria anticipated this and sidestepped the man, tripping him as his body fell past her. The attacker sprawled out on the sidewalk and clutched his battered arms.

"What's next, Christoff?" Marks beckoned.

There was only the sound of silence as Christoff considered his options.

"You let your women do your fighting for you, Marks?" he asked.

"Both of these women love this combat stuff. My wife has put four men in the hospital, and your driver gave her the opportunity to test out her latest toy. The young female bodyguard standing in front of me has already killed two men in a gun battle who were trying to get their hands on us. She could kill all three of you before you got your guns out. Whose bonehead idea was this?" asked Marks.

Christoff said nothing.

"I suppose you want to tell me to butt out of the military budget. What were you planning on doing – threatening and roughing us up? I don't think you're in a position to do either, unless you want to risk getting someone killed in a street fight. I suggest you pick up your driver and go back home to Baltimore," said Marks.

"You don't know what you're up against, Marks," said Christoff.

"Maybe, but it's clear that neither do you. Get in your van and take your two brothers with you while you still can."

CHAPTER 15: LEVERAGE

Marks had to wait two weeks for his appointment with Majority Leader Clifton Kellogg, then another 30 minutes in the lobby. When he was finally ushered into the office, Kellogg was on the phone. He waved Marks in and motioned for him to take a seat. While waiting for the phone call to end, Marks wrote a short note in ridiculously small handwriting and laid it on the desk directly in front of Kellogg. It read:

Your phone is bugged and there's a surveillance camera looking over your shoulder. Let's go to lunch!

Kellogg glanced up at Marks and said into the phone's receiver, "Just a minute." He leaned over to read the note. His eyes widened as he looked at Marks then back down at the note. Kellogg covered it with his hand and stuffed it in his suit's breast pocket.

"Bob, I'll have to call you back," he said before hanging up. Kellogg stared at Marks for over a minute, processing the implication of the note. Marks nodded affirmatively several times.

"It's 'Marks', right?"

"Yes, sir. Cliff Marks from the 5th Congressional District of Missouri."

"Thanks for the information. I'll give it some consideration...after I've eaten. I'm hungry. How about some lunch?" Kellogg asked, briskly leading Marks out of his office.

"We're going to lunch at Marcel's," Kellogg announced to his staff, as he charged out of the office and into the hallway, with Marks's two security guards right behind them. "I have a reserved table at Marcel's," he told Marks.

Kellogg, who was skeptically surveying Alexis and Chad, pointed his right index finger toward them. He turned to Marks and asked, "Who are these people? They don't look like staffers."

"Bodyguards. Come on, my car's out front," Marks answered.

As they walked down the Capitol's front steps, Marks noticed Gloria standing next to their car. She was talking with a cop, who was writing her a citation for being illegally parked.

"What kept you guys? He was about to call for a tow truck," Gloria smiled as she took Kellogg's offered hand. "I'm Gloria Marks. My husband told me of his discovery in your office. Glad you could join us for lunch."

She purposedly stood a little too close to Kellogg, brushing his shoulder with her chest and giving him her sexiest smile. She was doing everything she could to keep him off balance.

Kellogg looked back and forth from Marks to Gloria, totally baffled by the day's events.

"After the note from your husband, I couldn't refuse," Kellogg replied. In awe of Gloria's beauty, he continued, "Call me Kirk." He fished the note from his breast pocket and handed it to her.

The cop recognized Kellogg and stopped writing. "Have a good day, folks," he said, then opened the back door of the SUV. Kellogg and Gloria moved to the back row, while Marks sat in the middle row by himself.

Gloria led the conversation. "I don't think we should go to Marcel's restaurant, Kirk. Your reserved table is bugged. Your enemy knows you always sit there. If you can play hooky for a couple hours, we'll go to our home for a private lunch."

"Sure," was all Kellogg could say. He was stunned by the level of surveillance involved. After staring at Gloria's breasts several times, she whispered in his ear, "They're real," then poked them with her finger. Kellogg blushed.

Gloria's clothes never exposed any part of her breasts. They were prominent enough without calling more attention to them. She believed they lost some of their allure when exposed. Only her husband was allowed to see her bare chest, which she knew did not get him aroused. Oddly, though, her lips turned him on.

Gloria took everyone's lunch order and called it in to Gleason. She maintained a steady chatter throughout the drive until they reached Gleason's entrance. She became quiet to allow Kellogg to marvel at the scope of the grounds. Gloria instructed the driver to let them out at the stairs of the front entrance. Chad opened the back door for Kellogg and Gloria to exit. Marks and Alexis remained in the SUV to drive it to the underground garage.

Kellogg stopped next to one of the eagle statues at the front entrance and turned to Gloria. "They're beautiful," he said, catching himself staring at her chest once again.

Gloria laughed, "Thank you. They probably kept me from getting the gold medal – too much drag. When I quit training hard for the Olympics, I gained a few pounds, and most of it went up here. Someone once gave me a t-shirt that said, *'I see you've met the twins'*. I stopped wearing it because everyone wanted to hold them."

They were both chuckling when Carston opened the door and ushered them across the foyer and into the den. Kate O'Rourke was standing at the bar, ready to mix drinks. She even had a full bowl of Cheetos, Kellogg's favorite snack, on display for him. Marks ordered a Sun Drop soda, and Gloria ordered two margaritas. She knew Kellogg's drink of choice.

"You seem to know a lot about me," said Kellogg, picking up his drink and moving away from the bar. He had never been around a woman so candid. He immensely enjoyed Gloria.

After several swallows of his drink, Kellogg set his glass on the ornate coffee table and sat down in an overstuffed chair.

"I could sure go for a cigarette," Kellogg admitted.

"I didn't know you smoked," replied Marks.

"I have one or two a year, on special occasions. I don't see any ashtrays, so I guess neither of you smoke."

"Cliff used to when he was working in construction. He had a serious accident and was in a coma for over three weeks. I guess his body lost its craving for nicotine. He's only had two since I've known him: on our honeymoon night and on election night," said Gloria. "But our lease prohibits smoking inside the residence. Let's adjourn to the veranda. I think our beautiful barmaid can help you out."

"Yes, ma'am," said Kate O'Rourke, pulling a porcelain encased lighter and unopened pack of cigarettes from under the bar counter. She followed them onto the veranda that overlooks the pool.

"May I open the pack for you?" asked O'Rourke.

"Please."

She opened the pack and slapped it on her palm several times until a few cigarettes popped up. Kellogg graciously took one and leaned in toward Kate as she lit it for him. She then set the lighter and pack on the table. Gloria thought Kellogg's cheeks were going to bust when they collapsed inward from a deep inhale.

Marks knew Kellogg was loving every minute of this – being pampered by two beautiful women, having his favorite drink, and smoking his long-awaited cigarette.

"You can serve lunch out here when it's ready," Gloria directed O'Rourke before she headed back inside. She returned shortly with a pitcher of margaritas that she placed on the table. She topped off Kellogg's glass and disappeared again.

"Okay, long delayed…why did you want to see me, Cliff?"

"I need your vote on the American Homelessness Bill and support on how the program will be funded. I hoped that telling you about the surveillance of your office would persuade you to help me in return. If not, there are several other issues that are more serious that make you vulnerable to your enemies. I can help mitigate them if we can come to each other for support," Marks proposed.

"You know how contrary your bill is to my 30 years in the House?"

"Yes, and that's why I'm bringing a lot of meat to the table. Let's start with the intern you got pregnant 10 years ago. You gave her $20,000 to have an abortion, which is grossly contrary to your 30 years in the House. And guess what? You have a nine-year-old son," Marks stated.

"That's a pure bullshit rumor of yesteryear!" refuted Kellogg.

Marks retrieved a photo from his inside suit pocket and laid it on the table. The boy was the spitting image of Kellogg. Kellogg put his hand over his mouth to muffle his exclamation. He fell back in his chair.

Gloria and Marks waited.

"I didn't know. How's the boy and his mother?" Kellogg asked.

"They're fine. Her parents are rich. She got married and had two more children. Her husband was killed in Iraq," said Gloria.

"Any more revelations?" Kellogg inquired apprehensively.

"Yes, you're getting careless. Too many of the stocks you buy coincide with legislation you support that benefits the company's stock price. The Security and Exchange Commission is becoming aware of your activity and is going to charge you with insider trading. They know that the president of a drug company called you, eliciting your support for extending the patent rights of one of their most profitable drugs. In exchange, he told you of a major breakthrough with a new drug, which would be announced in a couple months...so now seemed like a good time to buy their stock, which was depressed due to the pending patent right expiration. You bought 20,000 shares at $25 each. The stock will probably increase well into triple digits if the new drug is successful. You could make a killing. My advice is to sell the stock and invest in a dividend stock as soon as possible. You may not know it, but the drug company used you. They desperately need money to finish their Phase 1 trials before they could start Phase 2. They won't know if the drug is successful for at least another year. They hoped you'd tell relatives and friends of your hot tip, which you did. In two weeks, over a million shares were bought, pumping over $28 million into the company. Anyway, there won't be a quick profit from buying and selling the stock. You may have a few pissed-off friends and relatives when they realize this is a long-term investment," said Marks.

"How in God's name do you know all of this?"

"I'm half owner of a detective agency. We make it our business to know about people. It's also why Gloria and I have bodyguards. You make enemies when you dig in people's backyards."

In truth, Marks had listened to Kellogg's mind when he sat behind him several weeks ago in the House cafeteria. Marks learned about Kellogg's affair with one of his former congressional staffers, as well as his illegal involvement in the stock market. Through his detective agency, Marks hired a stock market analyst to gather details about the stock trades. He asked Bonneville to personally lead the investigation of the staffer. He knew Bonneville would be discreet and not make any waves in the staffer's life.

"Do you have any *more* surprises?" Kellogg asked again.

"That depends on you. We've given you a lot of valuable information in exchange for your support. We're not threatening you, but if we can find this information, so can others. You're a more valuable target now that you're the majority leader of your party," said Gloria.

"Do you know who and when the surveillance cameras were put in my office?"

"A liberal Super PAC called One Nation. They were installed last week while the House was in recess, so they haven't seen or heard very much. I might want to leave them in place and use them to your advantage," said Marks, just as Carston appeared on the veranda.

"Sir, would you like lunch served here or in the dining room?" he asked.

"Dining room," Gloria interjected. "We've talked enough about business."

Two weeks later, Jerome delivered a note to Marks in his office in the Capitol. It read:

I'll make sure your bill gets out of committee and that my caucus won't oppose it. — Kirk

---

The next target to gain leverage for support of his bill was Congresswoman Judy Cook, a young outspoken, controversial, and charismatic firebrand from New York City. With her classic runway model looks, she was in demand for appearances on evening newscasts and talk shows. Not only was Cook easy on the eyes, she was also a gifted speaker who spoke with conviction and passion. Marks wanted her on his team.

He had met her once at a party caucus and knew she was still in the closet with her sexuality. Marks asked Gloria to invite Cook for dinner to see if he could garner her support. She accepted the invitation for a Friday night when most of the House members flew back to their home districts.

Marks sent their flashiest SUV to pick her up at her apartment. Carston and Marks were waiting for Cook by the underground garage's elevator. Carston opened the door and offered her his hand.

Cook wore a long, black wool cape and a dark green form-fitting dress with a split up to her thigh to display her beautiful legs. An 18-karat gold loop necklace adorned her chest, the matching black heels with gold tips on her feet. She had obviously dressed to impress her hosts.

"May I take your handbag and cape, madame?" Carston said in the politest British accent.

"Please," Cook replied.

"Welcome to Gleason, Ms. Cook. We can take the elevator upstairs. Would you like to see the residence?" asked Marks.

"If I'm not intruding on your privacy."

"I always learn something new about Gleason every time I give the grand tour," Marks explained, as the elevator doors opened to display the foyer.

"I think the foyer is the most impressive part of the building. In the old days, when ballroom dancing was in vogue, the foyer was the perfect venue – not only because of its size, but the acoustics are also amazing. Open hallways circle the second and third floors that look down on the dance floor. The stairways to the upper floors are located in adjoining rooms, so the length of the foyer isn't obstructed. I'm told by the older staff members that dinner for 100 has been served in the foyer."

"Your wife isn't here? I was hoping to meet her," Cook said, disappointment in her voice.

"I think she's in the den, having her daily ration of Jack Daniel's."

"Sounds like a good idea. We should join her," said Cook.

"Carston, tell Mrs. Marks we'll be joining her momentarily for a drink."

"I hope we can talk a little business after dinner. I'm seeking support for something," said Marks.

"Certainly. The majority leader told me about your agenda. The payment part is the big hurdle."

"Understood. Let's go find Gloria."

Gloria knew how Cook embraced fashion and wore the latest trends, so she splurged on an outfit for this occasion. Even to Marks, who saw her nearly every day, she was strikingly gorgeous.

Marks noticed that Cook was also taken aback by Gloria's stunning appearance. Her thick, black hair was swept up on top of her head, a style that accented her elegant neck. Her dark blue dress showed off her slender waist and broad shoulders. The slit on the side of her skirt exposed her long legs and gold spiked heels when she moved.

"I'm building up my courage to match wits with Congresswoman Cook," said Gloria, winking at Cook and holding up her empty glass, signaling a refill. "From what I've seen of your speeches, I don't stand a chance."

"You're too kind, Gloria," Cook blushed.

Kate O'Rourke approached them with a tray of drinks. A gin and tonic for Cook, a Sun Drop soda for Marks, and another Jack Daniel's for Gloria.

"Is a gin and tonic good for you?" O'Rourke asked Cook.

Cook took a sip and replied, "Perfect, thank you."

Gloria dismissed Kate.

"Cliff, how did you beat off Gloria's many suitors to catch her?"

"Two lost souls caught each other," Gloria answered, taking Cliff's arm.

"Well said, wife," Marks stated.

"Why haven't you found a lost soul to share your life with, Judy?" asked Gloria. "You know, someday, you'll have to reveal yourself. Most voters don't care if you're gay, especially being a lesbian."

Cook flinched, stepped back, and looked dumbfoundedly at Gloria.

"You're among friends, Judy. Me, I've got one foot in and the other out, which is easy, since I married a man. You, not so much."

Cook downed her drink. "I could use another."

"I'll get it," Marks said.

"You must have to beat off all the women," Gloria suggested.

"Some days, it's hard…but I sure miss a warm body next to me," Cook said.

"If you need company or to relieve the pressure, you're more than welcome to call me or come by."

Marks returned with a double gin and tonic. Cook was silent as she consumed most of the drink. "Can we go outside?"

Gloria took her arm and they walked outside and around the pool, each with a drink in hand.

"Were you serious about me coming by anytime?"

"I'm looking forward to it. Hell, you can stay tonight. Cliff won't care. We sleep in different rooms because he snores. We can have dinner, dance, swim, and make love."

"I can't believe this is happening," Cook responded.

"Let's have dinner and relax."

Cook marveled at the seven-course dinner with three different wines paired with the meal.

"Carston, please extend my appreciation to the kitchen staff. I've never seen or eaten a better dinner or had greater service. Five stars," said Cook.

"High praise, thank you. Would you like dessert and coffee in the den?"

"Please," Cook answered, just as Carston pulled her chair back as she stood.

Marks watched the women, arm in arm, sashay toward the den. He marveled at how he had reached the place where he could hang out with two beautiful women. *This must be a movie,* he thought and chuckled to himself.

Gloria had scripted the evening. Cook did not leave Gleason until 6 a.m. the following day.

Alexis, who drove Cook home, wanted to return to Gleason in time to eat breakfast with Marks.

Judy Cook had other plans. "Alexis, take me over to Georgetown, if that's alright," she added, not wanting to sound pushy. "Head for 30th and Olive. I need to see a reporter before she goes to work at *The Washington Post*. We'll only be there a few minutes…then I need to stop at a floral shop to send Cliff and Gloria some flowers and a card. Last night was magical in so many ways."

"You said 'We'," said Alexis.

"Yes, I want you to come in with me. It's still dark and I feel safer being with you."

Luckily, they found a parking spot near the reporter's brownstone. The lights were on as they approached the house. Their knock on the door was quickly answered.

"Congresswoman Cook, this is an unexpected visit. Come in," said the reporter.

"I borrowed Alexis; she's a bodyguard for Congressman Marks. I spent the evening at their home. I came by to give you the story I'll be telling my constituents today in my weekly newsletter: I'm gay. Cliff and Gloria Marks encouraged me to be transparent with the people who elected me to office. It's always been painful for me to not do so. You can call me if you need any further information for your column tomorrow."

"Judy, most of your voters came to the conclusion a long time ago that you were gay," the reporter mentioned.

"Maybe so, but I never said it. You understand, I never said I was gay. I couldn't make the words come out of my mouth. Fear of rejection and a profound lack of courage on my part," said Cook, as tears welled in her eyes and her voice cracked. "Take me home, Alexis."

Alexis put her arm around Cook's shoulders and ushered her to the SUV. The ride to Cook's apartment was silent until they pulled into the condo's underground parking.

"Alexis, come up and have some coffee with me before you drive back. You've been up all night waiting to drive me home. Please, I insist."

Cook owned a modern condo with classic decor, paintings, and photos. She threw her black cape over a hallway chair and led the way into the kitchen, where she made coffee and defrosted frozen pastries in the microwave.

"I've got to get out of this dress," said Cook, heading for the bedroom. By the time she returned in flannel pajamas, Alexis had already eaten a pastry and poured a second cup of coffee.

"Alexis, how did you get in the bodyguard business?"

"Well, I was an Army ranger, one of the few women to make it through that crucible. I had a couple combat tours and had applied to go to officer candidate school. Unfortunately, I got T-boned in a car accident and screwed up my left leg. I was medically discharged, so I came back home to Kansas City. I bummed around for a while before answering an ad for security guards. It was for Cliff Marks. There are fifteen of us that provide 24/7 care for them and their home."

"I had no idea. I thought you were the only one. You like the job?"

"The best."

"Has Cliff ever made a pass at you?"

"No. He's a perfect gentleman and, by far, the smartest person I've ever met."

"What about Gloria?" asked Cook.

"You mean make a pass at me? No. She did kiss me once when I saved their lives in a gunfight. I tingled all the way down to my toes. I wish all men could kiss like Mrs. Marks. I can close my eyes and open my mouth, and still feel her lips," Alexis described while closing her eyes.

Instantly, Judy Cook's lips were in Alexis's mouth and she was sitting on her lap.

"You suppose I can borrow you for a little longer?"

"Here to serve."

Alexis's cell phone woke her up two hours later. It took her a minute to untangle herself from Cook's arms and legs. It was Chad.

"You okay?" he asked.

"Yes, the congresswoman wanted to me to take her to a few places. It was hard to refuse. I'm at her place now. She insisted I take a nap before heading back. I should be there in an hour."

That evening, Alexis found Marks when he arrived home from the House. "She gave me a note for you, boss. That woman sang to herself all the way home. Mrs. Marks knows how to throw a party, even for just three people."

"Heck. I went to bed at 10 p.m., Alexis, so it was just two women."

"Yes, sir. That's what I figured."

"You should've joined the party."

"If there is a next time, I will…as long as you won't fire me."

"Not to worry. You're permanent party, Alexis. There will be plenty of next times. This was just Round 2. Kellogg was Round 1 and Cook was Round 2. You'll be seeing a series of congressional members visiting Gleason, male and female, whose support I want. With my magical brain and Gloria's seductive beauty, we'll bend almost all of them to our will. You accidently became a part of that plan today. Do you want me to make you a member of the leverage gang?"

"Yes, sir! Sounds like fun," answered Alexis, who loved the feeling of being part of the family, especially when Marks referred to her as 'permanent party'.

"Some of the encounters may need you to go beyond your comfort boundaries to win the day."

"For you and Mrs. Marks, I have no boundaries."

CHAPTER 16: THE DEVIL'S DAUGHTER

Gloria was resting under an umbrella beside the Gleason pool after swimming 40 laps. She was waiting for her husband to return home from the Capitol building. She felt excited to tell him about what she had done at her trucking company over the past couple of weeks. She drank two bottles of water to rehydrate her body after the long swim…then requested her server bring her a Jack Daniel's cocktail.

Marks arrived as Gloria was ordering her second drink. Two weeks is the longest they had been apart since their wedding, and Marks deeply missed her company. After a long kiss, he opened the conversation.

"Did you have fun in Colorado?"

"I had a hell of a good time! I landed a new client, Summit Brick Company, in nearby Lakewood. They're expanding their business to out-of-state customers and were thinking about hooking up with a long-haul trucking company to make it happen. They did their own local deliveries, but didn't want to spend the money to buy semis for the long transports. I looked like a hero back at the company because I'm told that my brother had been trying to get into Summit for years. I got lucky by paying them a business call at the right time. More exciting than that, I did my first solo trip to haul the initial load of Summit bricks. I dropped off the bricks in Salt Lake City, then drove up to Hill Air Force Base, north of Salt Lake City, to pick up three jet engines to haul them to Tinker Air Force Base near Oklahoma City," said Gloria proudly.

"Damn, Gloria! That's a lot of miles," Marks replied.

"Yeah, 2,500 miles! It took me more than four days to get back."

"Holy crap! That's a hell of a trip for your first solo."

"The original plan was for me to transport the load out and come back empty, but the jet engine load popped up while I was on my way to Salt Lake. The operation center was going to fly a driver to Salt Lake to take over; I declined. The company would make more money if I took my time. I followed the law, which only allows 11 hours of driving a day, which equated to about 600 to 650 miles a day…so do the math. Plus, a lot of time is spent loading and unloading, and then doing the paperwork correctly to ensure we get paid. I was extra careful making sure the loads were secure. And I probably don't drive as fast as the company pros," said Gloria.

"Any problems?" asked Marks.

"Believe it or not, one of my tires picked up a railroad spike while going over a crossing. I was in the middle of nowhere, so I had to pull over and change a tire. All kinds of people stopped to help."

"No surprise there, Gloria. You attract men. Duh!" Marks laughed.

"I dressed down for the trip. I wore big overalls, a baggy flannel shirt, put my hair up under my baseball hat, and didn't wear any makeup," she said defensively.

"How about the truck stops?"

"Being horny must be a trucker's disease. I got hit on at the fuel pump, in the truck wash, and in the café – by men and women," replied Gloria.

"Could it be that they were just lonely?" inquired Marks.

"You're right, husband. Pardon my ego."

"The big sleeper cab certainly provides a convenient place for some shenanigans during mandatory off-times. Were you ever tempted on those lonely nights to overcome your fear of being bisexual again...before Captain Blackman, I mean?" asked Marks.

"You know," said Gloria.

"No, I don't. I turn my implant's receiver off to your mind unless there's a specific reason to connect with you," said Marks.

"Twice. I was blindsided the first time. It was my last day at Syntil, right before they placed me in the job at St. Luke's Hospital as an administrator for new patients. I worked late clearing my paperwork and collecting all my personal belongings from my office. I was carrying two big handbags full of stuff. As I turned down the hallway, I saw a woman standing by the elevator. She punched the elevator call button when I stopped by her. She let me go in first. I was tired, so I stood in the back corner and leaned against the wall. I must've had my eyes closed because suddenly, I felt her whole body pressing me farther into the corner. She said, 'You look like you could use a drink.' I must've agreed...but for some reason, I was concentrating on the aroma of her body," Gloria admitted.

"Body odor?" asked Marks.

"No, not that! I couldn't identify it, though. I opened my mouth and took a deep breath, thinking if I could taste the aroma, I would know what it was. I took another deep inhale to enjoy it more. While I was relishing the aroma, she pushed my hair back and surrounded my ear with her mouth. She sucked my ear into her mouth, and the tip of her tongue slowly swept over every contour of my ear. I melted. I dropped my bags and grabbed her around the waist and pulled her even closer."

"She asked if I wanted to go to her place. She still hadn't let go of my ear. I finally said, 'Yes', not wanting the feeling to end. She stepped back and pinched my nipples through my blouse. I didn't know they could get that hard."

"She said, 'We better hurry before you have an orgasm right here.' She smiled, took my bags, and pressed the button for the underground garage. She had a very nice apartment. She directed me to have a seat on the couch while she fixed me a drink. I asked her how she knew I liked JD. She said she followed me to a bar to see what I drank and to see if I had any attachments. I told her that I'd never seen her before."

Gloria continued, "She only said, 'Black wig.' I then asked her how long she had been following me, and she answered, 'Three months. Following you was my evening entertainment. I didn't need to rent porn to get horny. I started breathing hard just watching you. Mainly, I wanted to see if you had any boyfriend or girlfriend attachments. You don't appreciate nor understand that your body was designed by Satan, as if for his daughter, with malice and evil intent, to cause the ultimate temptation to sin by even the most devoted puritan Christian. For you not to have attachments made me wonder if you couldn't decide on which side – male or female, or maybe both – you wanted to be on. Your beauty took control of me. If I wasn't following you, I'd wonder where you were. I felt stupid following you and even telling you this now, but your hook was in my mouth and I couldn't spit it out. I even started going to a personal trainer to gain some muscle tone and lose 15 pounds, so my body wouldn't turn you off. You ruin me for other women. I tried, but nothing happened.'"

"So, I said, 'Wow, you've been planning this meeting! Looks like from the size of my favorite drink, you plan on getting me drunk. While I'm still able to focus and talk, from what I can see of your body, hidden under your clothes, it must be fit. What else do you have planned? How about another drink?'"

Gloria continued her story. "When my lover returned with the drinks, she told me she had a lot of sexual toys and wondered if I had ever played with them. I said I hadn't. She pulled them out of the cabinet and took time explaining to me the purpose of each one. I asked her which one was her favorite, and she said, 'The big dildo, for sure. It has chocolate in its head. You can really enjoy sucking on it.'"

"I handed her my glass for another drink. I noticed she was walking unsteadily when she came back from the kitchen with the ice clinking in the glasses and a big smile on her face. She was planning on being the aggressor, but I took over that role. I pulled her down on the couch with me. I buried my face in her chest and breathed in her aroma. I wanted to taste her skin. I popped off the buttons on her blouse as I pulled it off, and I broke her bra strap. She inflated her chest and cupped her breasts with her hands, offering them to me. I sucked a big nipple into my mouth...first one, then the other. She squirmed to slip off her skirt. She knew what was coming. I selected the dildo from her pile of toys. She watched me as I put the big head into my mouth, tasted the chocolate, then put it in her gaping mouth. After she sucked out all of the chocolate, I slipped it between her legs and deep inside of her."

"She screamed, 'You're the Devil's daughter! You tricked me, you gorgeous bitch.' She moaned as she took the dildo in her hand and stroked it back and forth into her body. She wanted me to be on the receiving end of the dildo. Her orgasm came quickly. She lay still for a moment to catch her breath. I handed her the half- full whiskey glass, which she poured down her throat, while I had another sip of mine. She started to sit up and reached for my clothes. I grabbed her wrist and put my knee on her chest to push her back onto the couch. I said, 'Later. That will be the grand finale – when you get to see your ultimate goal, my naked body – but we have much, much more to do before then. Let's see what toy I can use next. I got it, the vibrator! It looks like you've never used it. It's brand new, still in its sterile wrapping. You bought it just for me. Part of your master plan?' I knew she was enjoying what I had done and could only imagine what I was going to do to her. She spread her legs as I switched the vibrator on and slowly inserted it. She closed her eyes and took short, panting breaths. I tasted her nipples again, finished my drink, went to the bathroom, and then to the kitchen to make each of us another drink, while the vibrator did its work. When I returned to the living room, the vibrator was on the floor and she was out cold. I can only guess that the booze, two climaxes, and the physical exertion from them did her in. I wrote on her bathroom mirror, 'Stick to beer. – The Devil's daughter.' I rolled her over on her side and left the apartment."

"Were you disappointed that your playtime was truncated?" Marks asked.

"No, I realized that she was a predator, plotting to have her way with me. Her scheme to have me played to my vanity, but it also pissed me off, so I turned her game around," said Gloria.

"Did you ever see her again?"

"No. But if I do, I'll ignore her. If she had kept her mouth shut about her planning, the day could've gone much different. It was hard to walk away from her. The smoothness and aroma of her skin pulled me in like an invisible force. Plus, I love to show off my body to see how I compare to other beautiful and sexy women...which she was."

"How did you compare to her, Gloria?"

"I have a slimmer and more pronounced waist that clearly separates my hips from the chest. It draws you in to put your hands around my waist. Nobody has better breasts than mine because these big puppies still defy gravity. I made good money at wet T-shirt contests at college parties until my mother found out and made me stop."

"Wish I could've been there," said Cliff.

"Love, you can see me in a wet T-shirt anytime you want."

CHAPTER 17: PRESIDENT SEATON'S VISIT

During his third term in the House, Marks met President Eric Seaton shortly after the American people elected Seaton as their commander-in-chief. Marks knew what the president was thinking, and then used that insight to act in ways that pleased and supported President Seaton. To avoid being regarded as overly agreeable, Marks chose certain soft issues to disagree with the president about. Over time, he discovered the president's ideas and passions.

Every chance he got, Marks pushed the president's agenda in front of the TV cameras. He was invited to appear on news and talk shows because of his profound ability to recall past events, quotes from other politicians, discuss any congressional bill at any level and in depth, and speak accurately on any issue, no matter how trivial or late-breaking the events were. He wasn't caught off guard by any question, so he was the role model for always being informed and congenial. He never failed to put in a word for homelessness when being interviewed or while appearing on talk/news shows.

Marks was sitting in his chamber seat when his cell phone buzzed. It was Jerome. *Must be important. He rarely calls me*, thought Marks.

"What's up, Jerome?" he answered.

"Boss, a young lady from the White House came looking for you. She's in the outer room, waiting for you to return to your office."

"From the White House? What does she want?"

"She'll only talk to you," replied Jerome.

"You tell her if she doesn't talk with you, she may as well go back to the White House," said Marks.

"Take pity on her, boss. I'm sure she's just following orders. I already asked who her boss was. She won't say."

"What the hell? Okay, bring her down to the House chambers."

"She won't. She was told not to be seen in public with you."

"Wonder what in the heck's going on? Guess I better come over and see what all the hoopla is about. Tell her I'm on my way."

About 20 minutes later, Marks arrived at his office to find Jerome and the White House staffer, Candice Pegg, quietly waiting for him.

"Congressman Marks, please accept my apology for interrupting your day. I work for President Seaton's social secretary and I drew the short straw to come meet with you," said Pegg.

"I didn't know I was that repugnant," said Marks, with a slight grin.

"Oh, no – not at all. The job is just a bit awkward."

"What is it?"

"The president wants to be invited to your house."

"Is that what he said?"

"No, but he's asked my boss several times about your house. She worked with him for over 10 years, and she knows when he's angling for something, but he won't ask for it directly. She knows he'd be so embarrassed if the media found out he was fishing for an invitation."

"I understand, but what pretense do I have for inviting him? I'm an unknown third-string back bench congressman. The president won my district by 15 points in the election, so he doesn't need my help. Plus, it would be pretty uppity for me to invite him and expect him to come. Why would he want to speak with me?"

"President Seaton was an architect before he got into politics. Gleason certainly has a remarkably interesting turn-of-the-century design. He'd love to see it up close."

"That certainly helps, but we still need a better rationale for him coming over," Marks suggested.

"How about having a fundraiser party?" suggested Jerome.

"Excellent!" said Pegg.

"Sure, we could do that. Like a hundred people? I'll have Margaret Koluccy get with you about a guest list. What timeframe are you interested in?" asked Marks.

"In three or four weeks, during the summer congressional recess. There's nothing critical on his schedule then. That should be enough time to plan the party," replied Pegg.

"Good. Gloria will be back from Colorado by then. Margaret Koluccy will call you as soon as she arrives here with a couple of her staffers from Kansas City."

"Thank you so much, Mr. Marks. The president will be pleased and so will my boss," said Pegg, as Jerome ushered her out of his office.

"Do I get to come?" asked Jerome.

"Jerome, you can come to Gleason whenever you want, so heck yes. I told you to come live with us. You'll be by my side throughout the whole affair."

The White House Advance Team and the Secret Service came to Gleason the following week to examine the layout and exits. They did not want Cliff's bodyguards to be armed during President Seaton's visit.

"How many people are you bringing?" asked Marks.

"Eight inside, four outside," was the reply.

"Does that include the front gate?"

"No, your people can handle that. One member of the president's office will be present with the guest list."

"Okay, you won't see my people except at the front gate."

The fundraiser invitation was sent out to a hundred wealthy donors, all of whom had participated in past events. A fancy invitation with gold leaf lettering, along with a food and wine menu, announced the evening's agenda for President Seaton's $15,000-per-person campaign fundraiser. Cocktail hour was to begin at 6:30 p.m., dinner at 7:30 p.m., and the 12-piece orchestra would play from 8:00 p.m. until midnight. Formal entry to the fundraiser would be sent out upon receipt of the donation; the event would be limited to 60 people. Checks started arriving five days after the invitations were sent. The goal was achieved within eight days.

Cliff and Gloria decided that in addition to the 60 guests who gave donations, they wanted to invite 40 more. They wanted to include some personal friends and diplomats from the embassies they had visited in the past. Marks even called his sister, Michelle, in Mississippi to extend the invitation to her. Gloria sent her corporate jet to pick up their guests.

Gloria sat with the president at the far end of the foyer, next to the orchestra, along with four donors. The seating assignments thoughtfully mixed diplomats with donors and friends. Stu Nichols and Bonneville Taylor, in handsome tuxes, were strategically seated with female donors. Margaret Koluccy looked like a movie star and was seated with single male donors. For business reasons, three of Syntil's executive members and their wives were scattered among the diplomats. Marks and Jerome sat with Gloria's parents and two diplomats from the German Embassy.

Carston hired and trained 14 servers to add to the three in-house servers, so that every table had a dedicated server. Seventeen wine stewards were hired to ensure guests were served the wine they had selected, as well as any other beverages from the bar. They helped the servers clear and reset the tableware and glasses after each course. Six bartenders, who were stationed at three different bars, poured drinks all night, while several additional servers walked around with trays of champagne.

President Seaton arrived an hour early to take a leisurely tour of the mansion before the other guests arrived. He had never met Gloria. He was, like so many other men, overwhelmed by her beauty. Gloria took his arm and led him slowly through each room on the second floor and down the elevator to the vast basement. When he saw the racquetball court tucked away in the far corner, Gloria knew he wanted to walk inside.

"Mr. President, would you like to go inside and hit a couple balls?"

"Yes, I would. I love this game."

"Come play whenever you wish."

"Play with you?" asked Seaton.

"Absolutely, you can play with me, Mr. President," said Gloria, giving him a sexy smile, complete with a head tilt, sideways glance, and a wink.

"It must get dark back here when the lights are turned off."

"Pitch black," Gloria replied, flicking the light switch off.

Gloria led President Seaton to the front entrance right before the first guests arrived. She stood next to him, Cliff on his right, to receive and introduce Michelle, Jerome, and their guests. When the last guest arrived, Gloria walked the president over to the bar to order them both a drink.

"By knowing everyone's name, you must have the same brainpower as your husband," said the president.

"Cliff is smarter. His brain is a newer model," Gloria laughed, knowing the president did not understand her true meaning. She and Cliff, along with their Syntil bosses, had debated on whether to inform President Seaton about their implants, so he could use their abilities to know when someone was lying to him. They decided to wait until they more fully understood Seaton, the man, and his politics.

The Markses were proud of how smoothly the evening unfolded. Only one guest, who must have arrived half-drunk, started giving a server a hard time when he was told he was not allowed to smoke. The server raised her arm, the prearranged signal for help. Jerome and a security guard saw her extended arm and began walking toward her. Marks was right on their heels.

"Dave Clark, how are you doing?" Marks asked. He knew Clark had a reputation for being an obstinate cuss, but Marks knew Clark was a self-made millionaire, so he wasn't stupid.

"What the shit, Marks? You would think for 15,000 bucks, I'd be given the courtesy of being allowed to smoke a cigarette," Clark demanded, but in an increasingly softer voice, as he noticed two big men walking his way.

"Sorry, Mr. Clark, but no smoking is a condition of my lease with the owner, Mr. Gleason," said Marks.

"Hell, I thought you owned the place, Marks."

"Dave, I can hardly afford the electric bill. We get to live here for free just to make sure the house is maintained while the owner is gone. Anyway, you can smoke outside on the veranda or the front steps…or I'll refund your money and you can leave."

"I sure don't want to miss out on all the good food and beautiful women," Clark said, staring at Margaret Koluccy. "I guess the best option is to sit down and shut up. Sorry, folks," he said, turning to the server and the other guests seated at his table, "nicotine is a demanding mistress."

"Thanks for being a good sport," Marks swiftly replied, as he and Jerome returned to their table.

"I'm taking your sister out on the town after dinner. Okay, boss?" asked Jerome.

"Have fun."

The president gave a short speech after dinner, thanking everyone for coming. He mingled with the crowd for about 30 minutes and left when the band started playing dancing music.

After the last guest departed, Gloria and Cliff went to the kitchen. The army of hired servers and wine stewards packed the normally spacious area. They were wolfing down the leftover food and guzzling champagne from half-empty bottles, getting their fill before heading home. Gloria thanked them for the top-notch performance and applauded the chefs for the exceptional food. They told Carston he did an excellent job organizing the additional servers.

"I saw a lot of empty plates and full glasses, thanks to each of you. The guests were obviously pleased because I saw them leave generous tips at their table. How much was the total haul, Carston?" asked Gloria.

"It averaged out to be $250 per table…so everyone, including the kitchen staff, gets an extra $110," he announced.

"And my tightwad husband is going to match that amount," Gloria exclaimed, which earned a lot of yelling and clapping from the staff.

Gloria and Cliff took a tray of freshly brewed coffee and leftover dessert to the den to relax and discuss the evening's events before going to bed.

"I wonder where Margaret is?" she asked Cliff.

"Believe it or not, security told me she left with Dave Clark around 10:00 p.m.," said Marks.

"Come on!" questioned Gloria.

"For real. I saw them dancing. It looked like Dave had sobered up a bit after he got some food in him. They were very smooth on the dance floor and had an extensive dance step repertoire – from line dancing to the shag. I'm not surprised about Margaret, but Dave Clark…damn! He was amazing until I looked up his holding companies. He owns over 500 dance studios that teach ballet, tap, chorus line, ballroom, country western, and modern dance. In his younger years, he was a dance instructor and choreographer. He picked the right partner because

Margaret didn't miss a step. They looked like they were having a great time and had some chemistry," said Marks.

"I can't wait to talk with her," Gloria replied.

"How did the president enjoy the tour?"

"It was much more than he expected. When I opened a concealed wall panel to show the hidden passageway, he was dumbfounded. He had to step inside and close the panel. The second showstopper was the racquetball court. I knew he wanted to go inside. So, I turned on the lights and he hit a couple balls. I told him he could play whenever he wanted. He asked, 'Play with you?' I told him he could play with me anytime, and I gave him my sexiest look, wink, and smile. He got an instant erection and wanted to know if the court was dark when the lights were turned off. I told him it was pitch black…then I switched off the lights. I put my hand between his legs, told him he had a nice racquet, and asked if he'd let me play with it someday. I could hear and feel him breathing. He started to put his hands around my waist. I told him we didn't have time to play a full game and that I wanted to wait – savor the moment, you know? I pushed him away, turned on the lights, and walked out."

"You are the Devil's daughter, Gloria," Marks said, smiling at his wife.

CHAPTER 18: CHIEF OF STAFF

Marks was sitting in his House chair when his cell phone vibrated.

"Cliff Marks."

"Please hold for President Seaton."

After a brief pause, "Cliff, how are you doing?"

"Just fine, Mr. President. How can I serve you?" asked Marks.

"I need to use your super-brain lie detector," replied President Seaton.

"Where and when, sir?"

"Come over tomorrow for my daily staff briefing at 8:00 a.m."

"Looking forward to it," said Marks.

Marks sat in the chair against the wall of President Seaton's office, quietly listening as numerous members of the White House staff presented their briefings. The president asked few questions. He did ask his senior domestic advisor how he was coming along with the outreach program to single mothers; he informed the president that his staff were making substantial progress in putting together a proposal.

The briefing lasted about an hour. After the staffers left and the room was clear, the president looked at Marks and asked, "Who was lying to me?"

"Your senior domestic advisor has no intension of doing an outreach program, and your chief of staff knows it."

"Why?" asked President Seaton.

"They think it would show your approval of unwed mothers."

"I'm trying to help the kids!" the president exclaimed angrily.

"They don't agree."

"That's what I suspected. They think they're running the show around here. They've been slowly getting under my skin. It's time for them to go. Cliff, would you be my chief of staff for a month while I search for a replacement?"

"Not sure that would be legal."

"You'll just be on leave to help me out. I'll call the Speaker."

The call to the Speaker of the House was brief. Seaton signed a letter, which appointed Marks as his chief of staff.

Marks headed to the security office, the president's letter in his hand, to obtain a new badge that would grant him unrestricted access to the entire White House. He then found the deputy chief of staff and directed him to organize a meeting of all key personnel in the large conference room in an hour.

Marks called Gloria to let her know what had transpired. She thought the job was great for increasing his visibility in Washington and in the House. "I'm sure having a House member as the president's chief of staff has never happened before. Cocktail hour will be buzzing about President Seaton selecting you. Cliff, you've just leaped from the outer circles of power and low visibility, and into the highly visible inner circle of power. Your name will be all over town and the news! I'm sure the national and local TV stations will want interviews. You should do them," Gloria affirmed.

"You're right. I'll give Jerome a heads up at the office to accept requests for interviews if he starts getting phone calls from television networks. Right now, though, I'm headed to a meeting I requested with the White House staff. Talk to you later, love."

After hanging up, Marks walked to the conference room, so he could listen to his staff's minds as they trickled into the room.

He selected Jessica Townsend to be his vehicle to introduce himself. He learned that Jessica was a source of inside information for a reporter at *The New York Times*. Marks placed a silent call to Syntil's operation center, directing them to locate and call the reporter from *The Times*, and to then have the reporter call Jessica at 11:00 a.m., when the meeting was scheduled to begin.

Jessica was seated at the center of one of the two massive tables in the conference room as Marks walked toward her. He asked if he could borrow her phone. "Jessica, my phone is dead. Could I borrow yours for a minute to call my wife? I'm supposed to meet her for lunch," he said, sighing and pretending to be apologetic for the inconvenience.

Her phone vibrated as soon as she handed Marks her phone.

"Jessica Townsend," Marks answered her phone, perfectly mimicking her voice, revealing another of his hidden talents. He continued, "Jerry, I can't talk right now. I'm standing in the middle of a big meeting with the key personnel. I'm not sure what's going on. Have you heard anything? Okay, I'll call you back after the meeting."

Marks had everyone's attention with his spot-on impression of Jessica's voice. He looked around the gathering of about 50 staffers and asked, "Can I answer the next phone that rings?"

Almost immediately, something chimed. One of the staffers raised his phone.

"Where are you from, Alex?" he inquired. Marks wanted to hear him speak.

"I grew up in the south, but I've been in New England for most my life," he replied.

"Alex here," Marks stated in a perfect Boston accent, with a touch of southern drawl. It was, again, incredibly perfect.

Marks continued talking with the caller in Alex's voice, "Look, Peter. All I know is that the chief of staff has quit, and some congressman is here," he paused. "No, I don't know his name, but he's wearing the pin on his suit coat that congressional members wear. He's taking the chief of staff's place until the president can find a replacement. Call me back in a couple hours. I'll know more then."

Marks handed Alex's phone back to him and walked to the front of the room.

Returning to his using his own voice, Marks said, "I'm that congressman. How many of you know my name?"

Four hands went up. Marks pointed to a female staffer with the raised hand.

"You're Gloria Ritter's husband."

"You're right. You were on the swim team with Gloria. My name is Cliff Marks, and I'm Gloria's husband. I represent the 5th Congressional District of Missouri. The president has just appointed me as his chief of staff,"

Marks switched from his natural voice to Jessica's voice as he apologized to her and Alex, "Forgive me for showing off."

He then continued addressing the group in his own voice, "I enjoy mimicking voices. It's a good way to get people's attention and lighten the mood."

Marks continued speaking. "We're here to serve the president. We aren't here to be the instant source of information for every reporter and talking head in town. We'll provide them information when we jointly agree it's to the benefit of President Seaton's agenda. The two former members of the White House staff had their own agenda, not the president's, so they're no longer employed here. President Seaton was kind enough to find them jobs elsewhere. If any of you cannot support the president's agenda, I'll write you an excellent reference; you can easily find another job in the government and private sector. Our loyalty is to the president. At the same time, we act within the Constitution and the law. And if there's any doubt in your mind, talk to the White House counsel and have him put it in writing. Any questions? Nothing is out of bounds here," said Marks.

"What makes you qualified for this job?"

"First of all, I know everyone here," Marks responded while walking slowly around the room. He pointed at staffers, calling out their names and job titles. He called out 15 names before stopping.

He took a second to catch his breath, then stated, "And I know each member of Congress and what their shtick is. Secondly, I can remember every single thing I see and hear, as well as who said it and when. I'm an extremely fast and comprehensive reader. Next, I know when people are lying."

"Why did the president ask you?"

"He trusts me. I know all the key issues, as well as the pros and cons of each. President Seaton knows I have in-depth knowledge of every piece of legislation or program that you're working on or that's been assigned to you. Politically, I'm in the middle of the road – neither left nor right. I think you'd call me a moderate. My only agenda is helping the homeless. Now, by close of business tomorrow, please provide me with a one-page point paper on the status of your work. My door is always open. Any further questions?"

"Do you own the big mansion you live in?"

"No. Gleason, as the mansion is called, has 14 full-time staff members and annual operating budget of over two million bucks, which you know is way beyond my congressional pay. The owner moved but didn't want the mansion to sit empty. Gloria and I were lucky to be first in line to live in Gleason and oversee its upkeep," said Marks.

"How long will you be our boss?"

"I can't imagine much more than a month. I have other commitments, but President Seaton asked me. I think there's a lot of people who'd like this job. There are several here that are qualified, but they may not have the stature to have any leverage with the heavy hitters in the other government departments or Congress. Being a junior congressman doesn't give me much stature, so I have to rely on hard, irrefutable facts to carry the mail, as well as my ability to know what people are thinking," said Marks.

"Are you saying you intuitively or literally know what people are thinking?"

"Literally. I know you logically don't believe I do, which I understand…tell you what. Write a number on a piece of paper and show it to the people behind you. It can be several digits long," said Marks.

The staffer excitedly scribbled on her notepad and held it up for the people behind her to see.

"4086 – that's your mailbox number at your condo," said Marks.

"It is!"

"Do it again!" one of the other staffers called out.

A different staffer wrote down a number and held it up.

"555! That's the height of the Washington Monument in feet. You've gone to the top several times," Marks stated.

"How do you know that?"

"I haven't the slightest idea," he lied. "But I do. I always win at Charades," smiled Marks. "My point is, tell me the truth, even if you figure I won't like it. If you aren't truthful, I'll know as soon as the words leave your mouth. Alright, enough of the parlor games, but...," said Marks, intently glancing at every set of eyes in the room, "what happened here stays here. This is a classified briefing, meaning the information is only for those of you in this room. President Seaton and I will determine when to grant access to someone else. If you ever have an important meeting and you believe someone's lying to you, invite me to the meeting. The truth will come out. I share my closely-guarded secret with this select group of you bright people because we have important work to do for the president and the country."

Marks pointed at 4086, the White House press secretary, and said, "Please provide me a handwritten list of everyone here that they received the, uh...let's call it the '4086 Briefing'...and have them sign it. Everyone stay put until the list is completed. 4086, you can take the list to President Seaton for his signature in case anyone doubts my authority to assign a classification. The document shouldn't explain what the briefing was about. Understood?"

There was a resounding chorus of "Yes, sir." They all knew they had an extraordinary boss who was more than capable of doing the job as chief of staff to the president.

The month flew by quickly. His implant made the job easy, with his instant recall of any issue and the logic and rationale for the administration's position. He enjoyed working for the president and the West Wing staffers, but he looked forward to returning to his seat in the House.

CHAPTER 19: HIGHEST BIDDER

The encryption light on his cell phone blinked and vibrated.

"Marks here," he answered.

Todd Clifford, the CFO of Syntil, was calling. *Unusual*, thought Marks.

"Cliff, I wanted to let you know that we had a successful candidate two weeks ago on the West Coast. We're going to ask Gloria to be with the candidate when the doctors wake her up. Molly Candle will be accompanying her to evaluate the integration of the implant with the brain. Gloria's mission is to get the candidate to join the program. If anyone can convince the candidate, it's Gloria. According to the operation center, the implant is fully activated."

"Great news, sir. Who's the candidate?"

"We believe her name is Tyka Packston, a 28-year-old African-American, who was involved in a traffic accident. She had a severe head wound and her left arm was crushed beyond repair. The Highway Patrol report said she was a hitchhiker with no identification, except a medical bracelet indicating she has sickle cell anemia. The driver of the car that picked her up was drunk and survived somehow. He lost control of the car while going too fast on a curve and ended up hitting a utility pole. Tyka was ejected from the car. She was only 30 minutes away from our surgical team. The doctors are going to keep her sedated until her head wound heals, much like they did with you," Clifford explained.

"What about Jordan and Marie-Claude?" asked Marks.

"They're hesitant about making that giant life change. After seeing all the threats you were and will continue to be subjected to, they became skittish about seeing if their implants will activate with the additional electrical input to the implant," said Clifford.

"If you need any help convincing them, let me know. On another note, maybe you should consider sending Gail Weber, my officer manager at the agency. Have you met her?" Marks inquired.

"No."

"Gail is African-American, a retired police officer, and her people skills are excellent. She'll be a clamming force and should be able to help Tyka accept what Gloria and Molly have to say. She doesn't need to know about the program. Those conversations can come after the three of them develop some trust with Tyka. This woman will be in emotional shock when she wakes up to learn that she lost her arm, not to mention all the other wounds she suffered in the crash. Let Gail be her Jerome. Of all the people in the hospital, Jerome was the only impartial person I trusted at first. Everyone else had a hidden agenda and lied to me, but Jerome didn't. I knew it and so will Tyka with Gail. If her implant's working, she'll know that both Gloria and Molly have a hidden agenda and she won't trust them. Gail should be the first person she sees when she wakes up," Marks directed.

"Sounds like a good approach, Cliff."

"Good. I'll brief Gail."

"Alright, getting back to the main reason for my call. During my prior life, I was an intelligence officer in the Army. One of my fellow officers, Nathan D'Oria, is currently the director of operations at the CIA. It's time to see what they'll pay for the capabilities of an implanted mind. I'm bringing Robby, along with you and Gloria. You all can demonstrate how this capability isn't a one-time, weird fluke," Clifford proposed.

"How much?"

"Perfect intelligence is priceless...$20 million a year for a full-time analyst, or 100 grand per interview, with a minimum of 100 interviews."

"What does Robby get?"

"His cut would be 25%, so he'd get $2.5 million, minimum."

"Sweet," said Marks.

AND THEN THERE WERE MORE

"The same deal applies if you or Gloria do some interviews on the side."

"I'll take some of that action. My utility bill is killing me," chuckled Marks. "I sure hope you trust this guy. Are you going to brief him on the future depth of the program?"

"Absolutely not! What's the expression? 'Don't look a gift horse in the mouth'," replied Clifford. I'll demand that Robby's identity is compartmentalized, with special access required from the director of operations to know his name and capability. The same applies to you and Gloria, as well as your connection with Syntil."

"When's the meeting?"

"Shooting for next Tuesday. I'll give you a call. Hope you like to fish," Clifford said before hanging up.

———————————

Nathan D'Oria owned a lavish 30-foot fishing boat. He handled it like an old sea dog as he backed it up to the pier, so everyone could climb aboard. Gloria, Cliff, and Robby wore ski masks to hide their identity.

The bait box was full, and expensive-looking rods and reels were already in the holders along the boat's railings. He steered the boat east into the open sea for an hour and then cut the engine off to let the boat bob in the water.

They followed Nathan down into the cabin while the two bodyguards fished.

"You have the floor, Todd."

Todd handed Nathan a typed sheet of paper containing 10 different short sentences. "No one has seen these sentences, except me. Read one of them to yourself, Nathan," asked Clifford.

Clifford looked at Robby. "Fishing can be a lifetime recreation," said Robby.

"Read another sentence."

Clifford looked at Gloria. "You read the same sentence, Nathan," stated Gloria, smiling and shaking a finger at him.

"Nathan thinks this is some elaborate game of deception. You write something on a piece of paper, and I'll tell you what it is just as fast as you can write it. Oh, and we'll all turn our backs to you to prevent any sort of cheating," Marks instructed.

"A storm is coming in, so we have to head back," recited Marks, as Nathan wrote.

"What the hell's going on?" said Nathan, giving Todd a confused look.

"These three people have the ability to read your mind and anybody else's mind – and as a bonus, they can do this in almost any language."

"That I've got to see."

"You're fluent is several languages, Nathan. What are they?" Clifford asked while focusing on Robby.

"Mandarin and Arabic," answered Robby.

"Think of a sentence in either language, Nathan."

"Roses are red, violets don't last as long, and you used Mandarin," said Gloria.

"You're blowing my mind. How are you people doing this magic?" asked Nathan.

"How is not for sale. Besides, what do you care, Nathan? In your business, this capability is priceless. Imagine knowing when someone's lying, what they're really thinking, and what they do or don't know. The person being interviewed doesn't know their mind is an open book. None of these individuals has to ask a single question; they only ask questions when there's an audience, sort of like a subterfuge. They just quietly listen to the person's mind. I'm here to give you the first chance to use it," Clifford paused. "We're also going to the FBI and the Justice Department."

"How much?" asked Nathan.

"At $100,000 an interview and 100 interviews a year, it comes out to $10 million per person per year. If you want him full-time for a year, the fee is $20 million. If you want exclusive use of this capability, the annual cost is $150 million for a five-year deal."

"You're kidding!" Nathan scoffed.

"I couldn't be more serious. Hey, look. Syntil has spent over $400 million to develop their mental capability, and we need to start getting a return on our investment. Hell, my annual operational costs are over $50 million. These three geniuses aren't free. Two are only part-time and are available when you need extra help. One can be full-time if the working environment is good. Your minimum cost is $10 million, due on the first day Robby shows up for work. None of this paperwork crap of me submitting an invoice and then waiting 90 days for the government to pay," Clifford stated, tapping his index finger on the small table in the boat's cabin.

"You're asking too much, Todd."

"You want to know where and when the next major terrorist attack is going to be? These three can help you find out with 100% confidence. You don't need a team of field operatives, analysts, and computer experts searching and searching."

"Your agency has six people you're questioning – and without much success," Robby interjected.

"Boat coming!" one of the guards called down to the cabin.

A small Coast Guard craft came alongside Nathan's fishing boat as he climbed up the wooden steps from the cabin to the deck to join the two guards.

"We saw your boat bobbing in the water and thought you might be having engine trouble," declared a young lieutenant.

"Just saving fuel," answered Nathan.

"A weather front is about an hour away. You should probably head in."

"Thanks. Let me start the engine and we'll follow you ashore."

Upon returning to land, Clifford asked Nathan D'Oria to call him if he would like to see a demonstration with an uncooperative person. "Everyone will be in town for a couple days. That's how long the offer stands," Clifford asserted.

After D'Oria left the boat ramp and drove off in his car, Gloria, Cliff, and Robby removed their ski masks. "He doesn't believe us," said Gloria.

Marks and Robby nodded their heads in agreement.

"He thinks you're in a financial bind and will come down in price. He won't be calling you. He knows we won't go public to make him look bad. He plans to wait you out," said Marks.

"How long?"

"Since he's really skeptical about the broad-based use of our ability, he doesn't feel any pressure to pass up using us."

"Todd, do you have an alternative plan?" asked Gloria.

"I didn't think one would be necessary," he replied.

"Do you care if D'Oria gets in trouble?" asked Marks.

"What do you mean?" asked Clifford.

"Wonder what would happen if D'Oria's boss found out he passed up a golden opportunity for perfect intelligence and didn't even tell him? I'll inform the president and he'll call in the head of the CIA, who will be blindsided, pissed, and embarrassed because it'll look like he didn't know what was going on within his own agency. Shit will hit the fan, guaranteed," Marks predicted.

"I don't know if the president was briefed on the program," said Clifford.

"He's not, he only knows about my ability. Walt Champion wanted to see if we could trust the president to protect my identity and ability. I know he hasn't told anyone. The president views it as a secret weapon to be used when he wants me to check the veracity of his staff and appointees."

"Has he asked you to use it on his staff?"

Marks paused before answering. "Yes, once. You may have heard it on the news – his senior political advisor and chief of staff took jobs in the private sector. One was lying and the other was covering it up. The president suspected it and I confirmed it. He confronted them and they both apologized and resigned."

"So, that's how you became the interim chief of staff until the president found a replacement?"

"Yep! He wanted me to quit the House and be full-time. I told him there's not a chance in hell…but I sure had fun jerking his prima donna staff around for a month," said Marks.

"Okay, we'll play chicken with D'Oria for a week, and then you talk to the president if D'Oria doesn't blink," said Clifford.

"Sounds like fun," Gloria added.

"Mr. President, what can I do for you?" asked Beck Lambert, director of the CIA.

"Beck, I had an extraordinary conversation with someone who can read people's minds…and I don't mean guess or have a good idea. I mean, they know *exactly* what a person's thinking, word for word."

"That does sound extraordinary, sir."

"The person knows when you're lying – and get this – in almost every language. I didn't believe it until I watched it happen. You know I speak fairly good German; the person knew what I was thinking in German! The person came to me because that capability was offered to the CIA and was turned down. I was shocked. What was your rationale for not wanting that capability?"

Lambert, stunned that the president had better information than he did, took a moment before he could reply. "Mr. President, I'm sorry, but this is all news to me."

"Hmmm, I would think this kind of information would find its way to your desk, Beck," President Seaton replied, an incredulous tone in his voice.

"Yes, sir. It should have," said Lambert, who was becoming angry that the president had better intelligence than him. "Sir, do you know who this person spoke with at the CIA?"

"Ah, the name reminded me of a cookie." The president enjoyed having the upper hand on Lambert, who he regarded as somewhat of an arrogant snob.

"Mr. President, can you tell me who you talked to?"

"No, I have to protect this person's identity. Several violent kidnapping attempts have already been made, so the strictest control of this information is paramount, Beck. You can imagine how many different countries and organizations would kill for this capability...if they couldn't capture the person, they could kill him, so no one else could use his ability. We don't need to hear about this in *The New York Times*. Get back to me as soon as you can run down this cookie guy. We need this person on our side, whatever the price," President Seaton directed before hanging up the secure landline phone on his desk.

———————————

Lambert pounded his fists on his desk as the cookie man, Nathan D'Oria, stood on the other side of it.

"What the hell were you thinking?" demanded Lambert.

"But, sir. They wanted $150 million a year for five years."

"You knucklehead! I don't care if they wanted $500 million. Pull your head out of your ass! We don't need this capability to fall in the hands of China or Russia. Who is this person?"

"Todd Clifford is the chief financial officer for Syntil Corporation in Kansas City. He had three people with him, who were wearing ski masks and who have this strange capability. I thought the company was in a financial bind to recoup some of their investment and would come down in their offer if I waited him out," said D'Oria.

"For Christ's sake, Nathan!" yelled Lambert. "We're not the only game in town or in the world. Call Clifford back and tell him he has a deal – now! I want to meet with these people."

"Cliff, your conversation with the president worked. D'Oria just called to say we have a deal. The head of the CIA wants to meet everyone. I'm not sure how, where, or if we should do that," said Clifford.

"I can understand why he wants firsthand proof; it's a lot of money. I think we should all arrive at the CIA headquarters separately and when most people are coming to work. Have D'Oria get you four security passes so we can walk in like we work there. Their security system will know when we arrive and someone will escort us to where they want to meet," Marks instructed.

Clifford, Gloria, Marks, and Robby were taken to a secure conference room and waited. After about 10 minutes, Lambert joined them and took a seat at the head of the table. Nathan D'Oria, director of operations, was not with Lambert.

"Mr. Lambert, I'm Gloria Marks, and this is my husband, Congressman Cliff Marks. And this is Todd Clifford, the CFO from Syntil Corporation, and one of their employees, Robby Crumpton," Gloria said in Arabic, which she knew Lambert spoke.

She switched back to English and stated, "Mr. Clifford is the only one of us who doesn't speak Arabic."

"Thank you for coming. To satisfy me, I'd like the three of you to separately interview someone who's currently detained and then record what you've learned. Will you do that?" asked Lambert.

"Gladly," Gloria answered. "I'll go first."

An hour later, all three had completed their interviews and submitted individually recorded reports of the interviews.

While the three interviews were being conducted and the associated reports finalized, Lambert stayed in the conference room and read some documents on his laptop. His computer registered each recorded interview's submission for real-time tracking. As he listened to each report, he nodded his head affirmatively and declared, "Truly amazing! I'm convinced. Mr. Clifford, I assume you're taking care of the business end of this arrangement?"

"Yes."

"As you can understand, it'll take a couple days to come up with the down payment of $10 million," said Lambert.

"You don't want exclusive rights?" Clifford asked.

"I can't commit to that amount. Ten million is within my authority, but $150 million isn't. It'll take some time to reshuffle internal priorities then get approval from the House Permanent Select Committee on Intelligence to approve the money for the next five years."

"If the committee approves the five-year funding, Syntil won't seek work elsewhere for Robby," said Clifford. However, let me be clear: Gloria and Cliff are free agents and will *only* use their capability in a positive way in the United States. Cliff has a standing consultant agreement with the Kansas City Police Department, and he interviews new employees for the US Attorney in Kansas City, as well as works with St. Luke's Hospital in comatose patient recovery. Gloria is new to this capability and has no commitments, except her large trucking company in Colorado. They can be available if you request their help. Robby is the only one fully committed to your agency – and you will be the only agency fully aware of the extent of their capability. Guard it carefully because their lives depend on that secrecy."

"I'm still in physical recovery from a car bombing intended for Congressman Marks, so this non-physical work of interviewing people is perfect for me. Under the master's guidance, I've been honing my skills by working at a detective agency and with comatose patients. And I'm gay," Robby stated.

"Thank you for your candor, Robby. It's my intent to gain exclusive rights to your abilities," said Lambert, as he got up and came around the table to shake hands with each person. "If no one has any objections, I'd like Robby to stay behind and get processed into the organization, so I can put him to work as soon as the funding's approved."

CHAPTER 20: SPEAKER

At the beginning of his four terms in Congress, Cliff Marks was well-known and respected in the House. He knew the in-depth details of each piece of legislation, its pros and cons, what it would cost, how much it would save, and which constituents would be affected. His fellow House members sought him out if they had questions about a bill. Congressman Marks was easy to find because he was always in his House seat. They knew he would tell them, in a bipartisan way, exactly what the legislation would and would not do, with no spin.

He had met and spoken with every member of the House over the past six years. He provided them with support and encouragement. A handful of the key members were invited to Gleason, where he and Gloria could apply whatever non-blackmail leverage was necessary to secure their support. He knew their pressure points and agenda, who was strong and who was weak, who was eager to serve their voters and who simply liked the idea of being a congressional member and took the path of least resistance. Marks had commitments from 150 House members to vote for the American Homelessness Bill. The bill would obtain funding from a tax on not-for-profit organizations and 25% from the general fund.

The bill would establish 80 Federal Homelessness Agency (FHA) offices, one for every state and large metropolitan area. They would receive 25% of their funding from Housing and Urban Development (HUD), who would hand over the housing for homeless people to the FHA. The offices of both agencies would be collocated to ensure an honest, coordinated effort between the two agencies.

The vote in the House was close: 221 for and 214 against. When the bill went to the Senate, it had President Seaton's support, making it pass easily at 60-40.

Two weeks later, in a landslide vote, the members of the House of Representatives elected Marks as their leader. Members of both political parties supported his election because he had demonstrated a profound knowledge of its complex operation and procedures, as well as a willingness to work long hours to garner support and successfully pass legislation. The national television networks interrupted the normal afternoon programming to broadcast this historic event. At 38 years old, Cliff Marks was the youngest member to hold the powerful and prestigious position of Speaker of the House. The 75-year-old outgoing speaker patted Marks on the shoulder and pumped his hand while handing Marks the large wooden gravel. Tears welled in his eyes as he took the gavel and bowed to the House members. He looked up into the overflowing gallery of a long list of friends and waved the gavel at them, inciting hoots, hollers, and applause from them. Every comatose patient he had revived was there, along with the Car Club members, the Syntil executives, the detective agency staff, the St. Luke's surgical team that had saved his life, and his political staff from Kansas City. Gloria, Bonneville, and Marks's sister, Michelle, competed with Jerome, Stu, and Margaret as to who could yell the loudest. Once the rejoicing died down, Cliff Marks, Speaker of the House, banged his gavel on the podium several times. He looked to the gallery and commanded, "The House will be in order."

And so it was.

CHAPTER 21: MILTON TANAKA

In the House chambers, Cliff Marks sat next to a representative from Hawaii, Milton Tanaka, a brilliant and amiable islander. After graduating from the Air Force Academy and completing his military obligation, he returned to Hawaii and became involved in politics. Although his surname was Japanese, the ethnicity was chop suey – a mixture of Hawaiian, Samoan, Filipino, Japanese, and a dash of Caucasian from his mother's side of the family. His father's lineage could be traced back hundreds of years, well into ancient Japanese samurai history. Tanaka was a natural people-person and could work a crowd as well as Marks. The two became fast friends. Besides her husband, of course, Tanaka was Gloria's favorite congressman. He was a frequent guest at Gleason. The Markses had vacationed in Hawaii and met Tanaka's extended family of uncles, aunts, cousins from both sides of the family, and his four younger siblings. Within the Tanaka family, his father only spoke Japanese. Tanaka told Cliff that he didn't speak English until he started grade school. Cliff surprised them all and immediately became a family favorite when this haole, a mainlander white guy, could speak fluent Japanese. When Cliff spoke Japanese, Gloria often struggled to control her giggling. Her infectious laugher spread throughout the whole Tanaka family, with everyone laughing and applauding – and even more so when Cliff began blushing.

Tanaka had been a House member for eight years and was an avid supporter of the administration. When President Seaton ran for re-election, he asked Tanaka to join him on the ticket as his vice president. After Milton Tanaka became the vice president of the United States, he was invited to a state visit to Japan.

The Japanese knew Tanaka was an avid hunter. On the third and last day of his visit, a pheasant hunt was arranged with a party of local hunters and officials. Beaters were used to flush the pheasant towards the shooters. As the honored guest, Vice President Tanaka was given the first shot when a pheasant took flight.

The 12-gauge over-and-under shotgun exploded in his face, severing one of his carotid arteries and the jugular vein on the right side of his neck. His right jawbone was completely missing. Metal fragments of the barrel penetrated upward into the bottom of his brain and downward into his chest.

The vice president was fatally wounded. His injuries were beyond the ability of his Secret Service agents to save his life.

A Japanese ambulance that accompanied the hunter party was called forward. Their efforts to stop the blood loss by applying direct pressure were unsuccessful due to the extent of trauma to his body. The paramedics confirmed he was dead.

The two Japanese foreign ministry representatives who had accompanied the hunting party wanted to move his body, but their efforts were thwarted by the Secret Service. This was a crime scene. They formed a human barrier around the body until the coroner and Japanese police could investigate the scene. The American ambassador, who came along only to observe the hunt, was visibly shocked. He sprang into action and rushed forward, as he also wanted Vice President Tanaka's body placed on the stretcher and safely rolled into the ambulance. The head of the Secret Service detail refused to allow the body to be moved, which sparked a loud and heated argument with the American ambassador. The in-your-face argument between the men did not end until the Japanese police arrived and took charge. After marking the position where each member of the hunting party stood when the shotgun exploded, they moved everyone back where the ambulance was parked and roped off the entire area in question. It took more than an hour for photographs of the death scene to be taken and all the physical evidence to be collected. Finally, to the relief of the American ambassador, Vice President Tanaka's body was carefully placed on a stretcher and the ambulance transported the body to a nearby morgue.

Marks was sleeping when he received a phone call from President Seaton's Chief of Staff, Travis Sloan, who asked him to come to the White House immediately.

When Marks arrived, the chief of staff informed him about the hunting accident and ushered him into President Seaton's office. The president did not look well. The shock of the death of Vice President Tanaka had a drastic impact on the president's numerous medical ailments. Marks had long been aware of the ailments the commander-in-chief had effectively concealed from the public. His type 1 diabetes and emphysema, caused from years of smoking, were now past the point of hiding from the public. A nasal cannula was fastened around his head and into his nostrils to provide 100% oxygen. Since President Seaton was in his second and final term of office, he was slowly letting go of his obsession to conceal his health conditions. The death of Milton Tanaka was a mortal blow to the president's plan of having Tanaka succeed him in two years, at the end of his term.

Secretary of State Sofia Aragon and Secretary of Defense Brewster Southerton were waiting in the Oval Office.

"Thanks for coming, Cliff. Have a seat. I want you to go to Japan to bring Milton's body back to America. You knew Milton and his family, and Milton told me they loved you. With your perceptive mind and secret ability to speak Japanese, I'm betting you can find out what happened.

Modern, expensive shotguns just don't blow up…yet I have no idea why anyone in Japan would want to kill him," President Seaton stated, struggling to breathe and keep his composure.

"It would be an honor to go. With your permission, I'll take Gloria and four of my people with me."

"Certainly. Air Force One is being prepared and will be ready to take you within the hour. Secretary of State Sofia Aragon would like to accompany you, but that's your call. I told her you're in charge."

"Who will the Japanese officials listen to? What's her agenda? What role will she play in our efforts to find out why, how, and who was involved? I envision her micromanaging the protocol and details of caring for Milton's body. I'm sure the chief of mission in the US Embassy is capable of handling those details. Her presence will complicate an already messy situation. Who will the flight crew of Air Force One take directions from? I know who the US Embassy will take directions from," Marks questioned.

"You speak fluent Japanese, Mr. Marks?" Secretary of State Aragon asked.

"I speak perfect Japanese. Milton and I only spoke Japanese when we were together."

"Why do you conceal that ability?"

"People say all kinds of things if they think you don't understand their language. I learn when people are lying," he answered.

President Seaton interrupted. "Cliff has an uncanny way of knowing when people are lying," he said, smiling matter-of-factly.

"Very well. I see my role in stressing to the Japanese government that the president of the United States doesn't believe this tragic incident was an accident. I'll tell the Japanese that you, United States ambassador-at-large, are specifically being sent by the president to investigate all aspects of the incident and that the president expects their full cooperation. I'll take the State Department aircraft and you take Air Force One to show the importance of your status with the president. The embassy will provide you with a list of all the Japanese people involved in the planning of and who were present at the pheasant hunt, as well as the agency involved in the investigation. I'll request that the Japanese official in charge of the investigation meets you upon arrival. And I won't tell them or anyone that you speak Japanese. Okay, Ambassador Marks?"

"I yield, Madam Secretary," said Marks, extending his right hand towards her. "Will you take Milton's parents with you?"

"Yes, that'll keep them away from your involvement with the police investigation," she replied.

"On your way, everyone!" instructed President Seaton.

"Tell the Air Force One commander that we'll be making a quick stop at the Kansas City International Airport to pick up three people. I'll bring four people with me from here," Marks told Sloan.

"Bring everyone here then the Marine helicopter can take you to Air Force One. If you have no objection to it, the White House photographer is coming with you," replied Sloan.

"Good idea," answered Marks.

Marks called Bonneville as he waited for Gloria to pack clothes for them. She collected Jerome and their two personal security guards, Alexis and Chad, and hurried to the White House. Marks told Bonneville about the trip to Japan and that he needed him, the agency's firearms expert and their forensic investigators to join them.

An hour later, Marks, Gloria, Jerome, Alexis, Chad, and the photographer walked across the White House lawn to board the helicopter.

With gut-wrenching emotions, President Seaton called Milton's parents just as the commander-in-chief, US Pacific Fleet, Admiral Swift, and Governor Channing of Hawaii arrived at the Tanaka residence. Milton's father subscribed to Japanese TV and heard the news of his son's death moments before the president picked up the phone to inform them.

Air Force One landed briefly in Kansas City to pick up Bonneville Taylor and Mike Branch, the agency's small arms guru, and Chester Spalding, their forensics expert. During the flight, they discussed how a high-quality weapon, such as the one used by Vice President Tanaka, could have exploded. They came up with two conclusions.

First, if the interior of the breach of the shotgun that holds the shotgun shell had narrow grooves cut in the metal of the breach, the grooves would weaken the breach's ability to contain the explosive force of the shell when the gun is fired. The force of the exploding shell would blow out the metal sides of the breach and into the person holding the shotgun and anything near the shotgun. The explosion would send potentially lethal metal fragments of the breach in every direction. Second, the shotgun shells were filled with additional gunpowder. The subsequent additional explosive force of the gunpowder might exceed the safety specification of the weapon to be able to contain the force of the explosion within the gun. The metal of the breach would break and blow outward, sending metal fragments everywhere.

Mike Branch believed these two conditions were the reason the shotgun exploded in Milton's face. They would need to see the shotgun and unused shells to prove this theory.

Gloria and Cliff used the implant's software language computers to practice their Japanese on each other during the long trip. It still made Gloria giggle when her husband spoke Japanese.

It was early morning when Air Force One landed in Japan. The chief of mission of the US Embassy was the first person allowed to come aboard. Marks gave Jerome the job as gatekeeper at the bottom of the aircraft ramp.

"Ambassador Marks, Mrs. Marks, I'm Sheldon Mavin from the US Embassy. I'm here to provide any assistance you may need."

"Welcome. Have a seat," Marks offered.

"The head of the National Police Agency and the police commander from the prefecture where the vice president died are here to speak with you. May I bring them aboard?"

"Sure, but don't come back with them. I want them to believe they can speak freely to each other in Japanese. I'll tell the big fellow at the bottom of the ramp to let them up," said Marks, as he picked up a small radio to inform Jerome. He whirled around to face Sheldon Mavin and said, "For your information, only – and I stress *only* – my wife and I speak fluent Japanese."

Alexis and Chad blocked the entrance of the conference room as the chief of mission led the two officers to the room. Chad asked him if either of the officers was armed and was assured they were not before he and Alexis stepped aside.

Marks and Gloria stood up as the two officers were directed into the conference room.

"Gentleman, I'm Cliff Marks and this is my wife, Gloria. This is my detective agency partner, Bonneville Taylor, and two of our small arms and forensic experts, Mike Branch and Chester Spalding. Chip Kirkland is the White House photographer and was sent by the president to record these tragic events."

"Ambassador Marks, Mrs. Marks, gentlemen. I'm Commissioner Mitsu of the National Police Agency and this is Commander Sigmoto of the Nagano Prefecture Police. The death of Vice President Tanaka is a national tragedy for both America and Japan. Our prime minister sent us to provide you any and all information surrounding the incident," said Commissioner Mitsu, in perfect English.

"Thank you. Who's the investigating officer responsible for this homicide?" asked Marks.

Mitsu turned to Commander Sigmoto and asked him in Japanese, "Who is your investigating officer involved with this case?"

Commander Sigmoto replied to him in Japanese, "Captain Hiroshe is in charge of the investigation, but I don't think it would be a good idea to allow the Americans free access to him. We need to control what information is passed on to the Americans. I'll provide the investigation report as soon as I have a chance to read and edit it."

"Captain Hiroshe is in charge of the incident, but he hasn't finished his report. I'll provide the report to you tomorrow," Commissioner Mitsu informed Marks.

"I don't want his report. We want to talk to him and see what evidence he has collected. I take it that you don't want us to speak with him," Bonneville implied.

"This incident is extremely sensitive, and the world is watching. We must be careful what is said and not said," replied Commissioner Mitsu.

"This 'incident', as you call it, was a murder. To believe otherwise questions one's credulity. As our president told us before we came to Japan, expensive guns don't explode. Unless you take us to speak to Captain Hiroshe right now, I'll talk to the Japanese press and media and tell them you're not being forthcoming," Marks pushed.

Marks's comment caused a rapid exchange of impassioned Japanese dialogue between the two officers. Sigmoto explained to Mitsu how important it was for the death to be found to be an accident and not murder. He would call Captain Hiroshe to make sure he provides only the information he is asked for, nothing more.

"Mr. Marks, we don't have a police protocol for how to proceed with this situation, so I'm being extremely cautious, which can, unfortunately, appear that we're not being forthcoming. We can leave for police headquarters now if you're ready. How many are coming?"

"Five. Myself, Mr. Taylor, Mr. Mavin, chief of mission for the US Embassy, Mr. Spalding, and the photographer. My wife, Mr. Branch, Mr. Sparker, and two security guards are going to the factory where the Citori shotgun is manufactured. The weapon is made by Miroku in the city of Nankoku, which is located in the Kochi Prefecture. My wife will charter a helicopter to take them there."

Sigmoto asked Mitsu in Japanese why Marks's wife was going to the factory.

Gloria smiled and answered in flawless Japanese, "Because I'm fluent in your language."

Both men were startled. They realized she knew Commander Sigmoto was biased and was not being honest. He was skeptical of her ability and tested her fluency by speaking to her in Japanese.

"A police helicopter will take your party to Nankoku, Mrs. Marks," Sigmoto stated in Japanese.

"Very kind of you, Commander. Please tell the factory that we're coming and what time we'll arrive. Is the police helicopter here?" Gloria replied in error-free Japanese.

"Ambassador Marks, a military helicopter will take your party to the Nagano Prefecture Police Headquarters. Are you ready to leave?" asked Commissioner Mitsu.

Marks called Secretary Aragon on his encrypted cell phone during the ride to the Nagano Prefecture Police Headquarters to update her on what he and Gloria were doing.

Aragon replied, "Cliff, the president is anxious to have the vice president back home and has decided to send him to the States on a military aircraft tonight. He thinks if Air Force One was used and left you behind, it would diminish your status. The US Embassy has arranged a departure ceremony this evening. You and Gloria should be there. President Seaton and the embassy are assuming you won't finish your investigation until tomorrow at the earliest. Do you agree?"

"I agree, Madam Secretary. Gloria and I will attend the ceremony. I'll see you there. We can call President Seaton tonight to report what we've learned so far."

Captain Hiroshe, who was responsible for the investigation of the death of Vice President Tanaka, gave a PowerPoint presentation of the events, during which he revealed nothing more than what was presented on the evening news. Mr. Mavin translated the presentation for Bonneville and Spalding.

Spalding asked who was at the hunt and where everyone was standing in relationship to Tanaka. Spalding assumed that if anyone in the hunting party knew the shotgun could explode, they would be standing to the left of the VP, or as far away as possible from the shotgun.

Captain Hiroshe glanced at his boss several times. He seemed uncomfortable, shifting his body weight from one foot to the other, while leafing through a thick folder of documents and photos. No one came to his rescue. After several minutes, he laid a group of photos on the conference table of all the people in the hunting party, as well as a labeled hand-drawn image of where everyone was located in relationship to Vice President Tanaka.

The manager of the game reserve was standing farthest to the left; he was shielded the most by the vice president's face and neck since the shotgun was held on the right side of Tanaka's face. The next person on the left was the head of the hunting lodge, the individual who organized the hunt. The prefecture game warden was the next person. The person to the immediate left of the vice president was the gunbearer from the hunting lodge whose job was to provide the shotgun and shells to Vice President Tanaka.

Spalding studied the photo at length and realized the gunbearer was standing in the wrong place. He reasoned that when a shooter holds a shotgun against their right shoulder, their body is slightly turned to the right. The gunbearer should stand to the right of the shooter to easily take the weapon from them and to hand them shells.

The head of the prefecture government was the only person on the right side of Tanaka.

"Was the person on the right side of Vice President Tanaka wounded from the explosion?" asked Bonneville.

"Yes."

"Were the metal pieces of the gun recovered from his wounds?"

"Yes."

Marks knew Captain Hiroshe was not going to provide any more information than he was ordered to, as directed by his boss.

Spalding asked, "Have all the pieces of the shotgun been recovered?"

"No," Captain Hiroshe responded.

"Why not?"

"They were standing in a very grassy field, so it's difficult to see all the pieces."

"Was a metal detector and magnetic rake used to find the pieces?" persisted Spalding.

"No."

Marks stood and spoke to the national police commissioner. "I'm ready to leave. It's obvious the Nagano police are withholding information. I'll tell the Japanese people, your prime minister, and my president there's a cover-up at play to protect the forces that murdered Vice President Tanaka," said Marks.

"The only forces at play are to protect the reputation of the Japanese people. I ask you, Mr. Ambassador, what is your intent – to rub our faces in this grievous affair?" Commissioner Mitsu implied.

Marks did not need his implant to know Commissioner Mitsu was angry; it was easily detected when he spoke.

"No, but at the same time, it shouldn't appear that our VP can be murdered, and America does nothing in response. Every country has dark elements in its society, as we have learned many times in America with the assassination of our presidents and civil rights leaders. I don't believe it'll be a disgrace to the Japanese people if an internal plot is uncovered," Marks replied.

"If his death was an accident, then no response would be required," said Mitsu.

"Suppose we work together to find the murderers and act off the grid as judge, jury, and executioner to dispense quiet justice? I'll join you in supporting the accidental death scenario. I don't think we could make that stick because too many people are involved. The truth would come out and then both governments – and your police – would be caught in a big lie. I'm not going to try and sell that idea to *my* president. Can you to your prime minister?" Marks asked Commissioner Mitsu.

"I think we can set that issue aside for now. Let's work together to find out who planned and caused the exploding shotgun. How would you like to proceed?" he replied.

"I want to talk to the four men who stood to the left of Vice President Tanaka. I want Mr. Taylor and Mr. Spalding to see the physical evidence, the shotgun, as well as the expended and unused shells. We need to examine all the shattered pieces that came off the shotgun; if pieces are missing, we need to go to the field to look for them with a metal detector and magnetic rake. Can you make them available?"

"While we're having something to eat, the police department will accommodate your requests," Mitsu stated.

The interview with the game reserve manager only revealed his concern about the impact the death would have on future use of the reserve.

The hunting lodge manager was worried if there would be a lawsuit against the lodge since the shotgun was considered property of the lodge.

The game warden was profoundly shocked by the death of Tanaka. He was afraid of being at fault for not inspecting the shotgun before it was used.

One piece of new information the police withheld from Marks was that the shotgun did not explode on the first shot. The shotgun was reloaded after the over-and-under barrels were fired. The shotgun's over barrel exploded on the third shot.

The gunbearer could not be found at his apartment or his gun shop. His two apprentices told police they had not seen their boss since the death at the pheasant hunt. The police canvassed his neighbors and reviewed his cell phone calls and bank records, which showed a recent deposit of over 101,000 Yen (the equivalent of about $50,000). Review of the gun shop's sales records did not show sales anywhere near that amount of money. The frightened man was found at a remote Buddhist temple and was taken into police protective custody.

Marks had left the police headquarters for Vice President Tanaka's departure ceremony before the gunbearer was found.

Bonneville and Spalding spent four hours at the game reserve looking for missing parts of the shotgun. Using the metal detector and magnetic rake, they found metal pieces as far as a hundred meters from where the vice president was standing. They laid out all the shatter pieces of the shotgun, so that Branch could examine them the following day.

It was dark and cold. A light rain was falling as the hearse carrying Vice President Tanaka's body drove onto the airfield and stopped close to the US Air Force C-17 cargo aircraft. An honor guard of a full company of Marines in Dress Blues stood at attention, as eight men gently removed the casket from the hearse.

Marks unfolded a handkerchief and laid it on the tarmac for Gloria to kneel on. Marks kneeled next to her as the pallbearers slowly moved past an assembly of American and Japanese dignitaries and the vice president's parents before fading into the interior of the aircraft.

Gloria helped her husband to his feet. She had never seen him so emotional. They stood embracing for a long time as the rain continued coming down. Secretary of State Aragon came over to the Markses, her aide walking beside her and holding a large umbrella. She hugged them both. She was moved by the deep feeling that Marks had for the loss of his friend.

Secretary Aragon and all the Americans who came to Japan in Air Force One and gathered in the aircraft's conference room. Gloria and Cliff changed into dry clothes and joined them.

Mike Branch briefed the group on the trip to the gun factory. He reported the company was very cooperative and answered people's questions. They stated that the model shotgun the vice president used had never had a breach failure or any other type of failure. A factory test caused a breach failure to occur when the shotgun was fired over a thousand times in one day.

The company agreed with Branch that a failure could be caused if vertical grooves were cut inside the breach. These grooves would weaken the circumferential strength of the breach. How many grooves, how deep, and how wide they were would affect how quickly the breach would yield from the pressure caused by a fired shell.

President Seaton took part in the meeting via a video conference with the White House.

Marks outlined the results from his conversation with Commissioner Mitsu and his interviews with some people from the hunting party. He then summarized tomorrow's work. Marks informed President Seaton of Commissioner Mitsu's desire to call the incident an "accident". The president agreed with Marks: an accident scenario could not be sustained, as both countries would be caught in a cover-up scandal.

"The truth must prevail," said the president before continuing. "Cliff, people were emotionally moved back home when you and Gloria knelt as Milton's casket passed by. Thanks to you both."

"We were trying to represent the best of you, Mr. President," replied Gloria.

"Thanks again. Talk to you all tomorrow," President Seaton replied, ending the conference.

The following morning, the entire American team and Chief of Mission Sheldon Mavin were taken back to the Nagano Prefecture Police Headquarters.

Gloria's team began a detailed examination of the shattered pieces of the shotgun, the remains of the shell after the shotgun exploded, the two shells that were successfully fired, and the shotgun itself.

Marks asked Commander Sigmoto if he and Gloria could privately interview the arrested gunbearer in his cell. Sigmoto agreed and escorted them to a holding cell down the hall from the conference room.

Gloria smiled and asked the gunbearer easy questions about his background and skills as a gunsmith, while Marks listened to his mind. It took over 30 minutes to fully understand the mountain of thoughts in the man's mind.

Vice President Tanaka's murder was a revenge killing resulting from an ancient feud between two warring samurai factions from the 17th century. The last killings in the ongoing feud happened shortly before the beginning of World War II. Both factions were almost wiped out by the war. The Tanaka faction left Japan and scattered throughout the world. The Kamoto faction stayed in

Japan. With limited resources, they sent agents after prominent Tanaka members when their location became known. The news that a Tanaka as prominent as vice president of the United States was coming to Japan was too good to pass up. The Kamoto family passed the hat around for money to set a plot to kill Vice President Tanaka. They bribed the gunbearer to tamper with the shotgun and load a shell with smokeless gunpowder above the shotgun's safety limits.

Examination of the shatter piece of the shotgun confirmed that grooves had been cut on the interior surface of the breach; the gunbearer apprentices admitted they had cut the grooves. This evidence, along with the $50,000 and the gunbearer's location at the time of the accident, was enough for the police to charge the gunbearer with murder.

Based on the description provided by the gunbearer, the police found the Kamoto family and arrested them on suspicion of murder.

Air Force One departed for home that evening.

CHAPTER 22: THE BEST WAY TO SERVE

On the flight home, everyone aboard Air Force One watched a recording of the ceremony of the return of Vice President Tanaka's body to America. President Seaton, against the advice of his doctor, was at the airport – and like Gloria and Cliff, he knelt on the tarmac as eight members of the US military carried the casket from the military aircraft to the awaiting hearse. The president's personal aide had to help him stand to walk the few feet to his car. His sadness surrounding the loss of Milton was noticeable in his movements and body language. The media (especially the TV stations that covered the event) discussed, at length, the president's declining health over the past two years since his re-election.

Barbara Seaton, the president's sister and companion, and who also lived in the White House, called Gleason the day after their return. She invited Gloria and Cliff to the president's personal quarters in the White House for dinner.

Since Gloria had not seen President Seaton as often as Cliff, she was taken aback by his shrunken appearance from when he was invited to Gleason. He had lost weight, his hair thinned, his body was bent forward, and his head faced downwards, except when he looked up to speak to someone. His normally commanding voice was raspy and shaky. He was now a man who believed his days on earth were rapidly coming to an end at the early age of 68.

When Gloria arrived, President Seaton remained seated in an overstuffed chair and offered her a weak smile. He was covered with a blanket and had a nasal cannula in his nose to supply oxygen.

"Good of you both to come. Have you met my sister, Barbara?" President Seaton managed to say before turning his gaze to his sister and asking, "Love, could you get Gloria a Jack Daniel's and water?"

"Certainly. Think I'll join you for one myself," she answered, moving eagerly toward a small wet bar across the room.

The president looked back at Gloria. "We never did get to play racquetball. There was always something more important to do. Thank you again for that wonderful evening. You both did the country a great service by solving Milton's murder. I was deeply touched, as were the American people, by the departure ceremony in Japan. I wept. The Japanese ambassador to America delivered a long letter of contrition today from their prime minister."

The president stopped talking to catch his breath. Barbara brought Gloria's drink, then took her drink and headed to the kitchen to finish cooking dinner. Cliff waited until President Seaton could speak again.

"As you can see, my health has deteriorated this year. I'm not sure I can fulfill the last two years of my term, even if I'm still alive. I need to select a vice president to succeed me. The only one I trust to succeed me is you, Cliff."

The president's labored breathing forced a pause in his speaking. He continued, "I understand that since you're Speaker of the House, you'd automatically succeed me if there was no vice president and I was incapacitated. I need a VP now to help me with the workload, so I can stay in office as long as possible."

Marks replied, "Thank you for the offer. Gloria and I feel obligated to consult with the people who helped me reach their goal of me becoming Speaker of the House. Gloria and I have unique talents, and we want to be in a position where they can best be used for the benefit of the country. I think I can serve in the House and be the Speaker for many years, longer than being president. I'm not a person who could be elected president of the United States. I have zero charisma, am not a gifted speaker...and I don't have the clean-cut good looks like you, sir."

"You were elected in your district very easily," retorted President Seaton.

"The stars were aligned. My wife's a local hero. I'm well known due to my successful detective agency that solved some high-profile criminal cases. I had several wealthy backers. The Vintage Car Club members supported me and knew the city. My business partner is the president of the Car Club. My excellent campaign manager is a local woman with a lot of connections. She knew what kind of politics worked in Kansas City. A large corporation had my back financially. My opponent in the general election was a crock, as were two out of three of my opponents in the primary. I'm a paid consultant for the city police, St. Luke's Hospital, and the US District Attorney. None of those factors would come into play if I ran for president after your term ended. I have no national reputation since I'm new to the role of House Speaker. The $8 million I spent for my election is chicken feed compared the money I'd have to raise for a national election, which I believe, is a terrible waste of money. I financed my own election and didn't ask for any contributions. Spending almost a billion dollars on an election is sinful when there are other, more pressing needs for our country. My heart wouldn't be in it – raising that amount of money by running around the country giving stump speeches and blatantly asking for money."

"Nothing says you have to run for election, Cliff. Just be my vice president. If you have to succeed me, you don't have to run for election at the end of the term. I need someone I trust in there and to take some of the workload," said the president.

"What about some of your Cabinet members?" asked Gloria.

"Most of the Cabinet members were selected for political reasons, not because I liked or trusted them."

"Cliff and I can tell you with great certainty that you can trust Secretary of State Aragon. She's extremely loyal to you, your goals, and is exceptionally smart. If you made her VP, she'd be a pitbull and take on anyone who didn't support you," Gloria explained.

"I haven't seen that in her," President Seaton coldly replied.

"She has stayed in her lane; you've never asked her to get involved in national politics," said Cliff.

"You're right. I never did ask for her help. My mistake. Would you broach the idea to her, Gloria?"

"Certainly."

"Cliff, if she doesn't want the job, will you agree to be vice president? Before you answer, you must know I don't have time or energy to go through the hassle of a lengthy search and vetting process, with all the different political factions pushing their favorite. I need someone who can hit the ground running. I'm not asking you to run for election after my term – just help me fulfill my term in office."

"I agree," said Cliff, reluctantly. "I need to meet with my sponsors to get their collective advice on your offer, Mr. President. Meanwhile, Gloria can meet with Secretary Aragon."

"Okay, that's settled. Let's see if dinner's ready."

President Seaton seemed to be in better spirits after their discussion, as evidenced by his healthy appetite during dinner. After the meal, the four of them played Bridge until Barbara insisted the president get some sleep. Gloria and Cliff took their leave shortly thereafter.

Marks called Syntil's operation center to verify they had recorded his conversation with President Seaton. He directed them to send the text of the conversation to the executive board and to inform them he was flying back to Kansas City and would meet with them tomorrow afternoon.

Lance Winford, the CEO of Syntil, started the conversation as soon as Marks had taken a seat in the executive conference room.

"Your rationale on why you should remain Speaker is in line with the company's long-term plans, Cliff. We didn't envision the sequence of events that would lead to you to becoming vice president or president, hence we were all caught off-guard by your conversation with President Seaton," said Winford, eyeing the other executives.

THE BEST WAY TO SERVE

"You must've been tempted to accept the offer. From rags to riches, then the presidency – that's one hell of a ride, Cliff!" said Walter Champion.

"With my implant's abilities and being married to Gloria, everything else pales in comparison. I have no desire to take that path. The presidency would be too confining. I'd have to give up my work at St. Luke's, where I can really help people in crisis…and make money for the company and myself. The same goes for the police department and the detective agency. All that would go away. It's too high of a price to give that up. I can still service the president. Just letting him know who's lying to him is extremely important."

"Is Secretary Aragon good for Syntil?" Winford inquired.

"I have no reason to believe she would be harmful. I think I can influence her, if need be. You might consider giving her a company briefing on the program if she becomes president," answered Marks.

"Would you tell her about your capability if she agreed to become vice president?"

"With your permission, Gloria and I would. To wait until she became president, then spring the whole program on her wouldn't seem right – like we didn't trust her with that knowledge as VP," said Marks.

"What does Gloria think of Aragon?" asked Champion.

"Gloria likes her. She's a patriot, hard worker, and has a good heart. Gloria is meeting with her as we speak."

Champion looked at the other executive as they nodded their heads in unison.

"We all agree with your rationale. Press ahead and keep us informed. By the way, great work in Japan," said Winford, leading the round of applause.

———————————

Gloria called the US State Department.

"US State Department. How can I direct your call?" answered the receptionist.

"Secretary Aragon's office," said Gloria.

"One moment."

"Secretary of State Aragon's office, how can I help you?" a female voice asked.

"I need to make an appointment with Secretary Aragon."

"Who's calling?"

"Gloria Marks."

"What's the purpose of your call?"

"An employment opportunity," said Gloria.

"I'll connect you with the Human Resources department. Just a moment."

"No, no. You see, I was told to speak directly to Secretary Aragon," Gloria insisted.

"Very well, leave your phone number and I'll ask her. What was your name again?"

"Gloria Marks."

Three hours later, the phone rang.

"Gloria, Sofia Aragon. I'm sorry, I just learned that you called. That won't happen again. Everyone is my office knows who you are now. Have you recovered from the long trip back?"

"Yes, thanks. President Seaton asked that I meet with you. Wonder when we could get together?"

"Just tell me where and when, Gloria."

"I've never been to the State Department."

"Sounds good. Someone will meet you at the entrance and will escort you to my office. Would you like to meet the Japanese ambassador? I'm sure he'd like to meet you. You and Cliff have become celebrities in Japan. I think a Japanese film crew is coming over to interview you both. Anyway, he's coming to see me in an hour – can you be here by then?" asked Secretary Aragon.

"Yes."

"Good. The ambassador won't be here more than 20 minutes. You and I can talk after that. See you soon."

The Japanese ambassador was startled when he spotted Gloria standing next to one of the chairs in Secretary Aragon's waiting room. He stopped and then followed Gloria as they were both ushered into the secretary's office.

"Mrs. Marks, this is, indeed, a surprise and great pleasure to meet you. Madam Secretary, you have me in your debt. I don't know how to repay you for giving me the opportunity to meet Mrs. Marks. I'll be the envy of our diplomatic embassy," said the ambassador, bowing and then extending his hand to Gloria.

"I'm sorry my visit to your beautiful country was so brief," Gloria replied in Japanese.

The meeting in Secretary Aragon's office lasted almost an hour, as Gloria answered question after question from the ambassador. The meeting finally ended when the ambassador realized he had overstayed his welcome. He handed the letter of contrition from the Japanese government to Secretary Aragon and took his leave.

"Gloria, he'll be boasting about seeing and talking to you for years," said Aragon.

"Just part of my expanding fan club," Gloria kidded.

"Count me in," Aragon replied, as they both laughed. They were silent for a few moments until Secretary Aragon asked, "Gloria, I wondered how you and Cliff learned to speak Japanese. Did you take it in college?"

"No. Cliff never went to college. We're both fluent in many languages. It was magical when we discovered we had this rare gift," said Gloria.

Secretary Aragon shook her head in disbelief, but said nothing.

Gloria spoke, "The reason for my visit is President Seaton is casting about for a vice president to help take on some of the workload that comes with the office. Cliff and I told him you could probably do that. The question is, are you interested in being vice president?"

"Wow, that came from left field! I never thought I was one of Seaton's chosen ones," said Aragon.

"Being loved and having the ability to do the job are two different animals. Also, he doesn't believe that he'll be capable or live long enough to complete his term. How do you feel about being president for the rest of Seaton's term and then running for election?" asked Gloria.

"Christ, Gloria! This is some heavy mail you're delivering. Am I the only one on your mail route?"

"Yes, you are," replied Gloria.

"What about Cliff? As Speaker of the House, he's more of a politician than me."

"Cliff doesn't want the job. He's a good regional politician, but not a national candidate. Plus, he'd have to give up his commitments in Kansas City. He did agree to take the job…but only if you decline."

Aragon rose from her desk chair and walked around her office several times as she mulled over the startling offer. She opened her office door and told her personal secretary to ask her deputy secretary of state and her chief of staff to come to her office. They arrived within a minute.

"Have a seat, guys. You know Gloria Marks?" They both walked towards Gloria and shook her hand before taking a seat.

She punched several buttons on her phone to call President Seaton's office.

"Secretary Aragon, is President Seaton available?"

"Madam Secretary, how are you?" answered Seaton, as he came on the line.

"I'm fine, sir. Thank you. Gloria Marks is in my office with an extraordinary request. My reply is that I'd be honored to serve you and the nation as vice president," said Aragon, her voice almost cracking from the emotions of the moment.

"Excellent. My press secretary will make the announcement in the press room within the hour. We can have your swearing in this evening, if you agree?"

"I agree, Mr. President."

"My chief of staff will arrange the ceremony and will get back to you. Welcome aboard, Sofia."

"My God! What a sudden change of events," Aragon exclaimed. Her staff congratulated her before leaving her office.

"One more thing before I leave. Cliff and I have the mystical ability, beyond being fluent in almost every language, to literally read people's minds. I know that's hard to believe, but we do. We know exactly, word for word, what people are thinking, what they believe, what they like and dislike, and if they're truthful or lying. We have a photographic memory, so we never forget anything we see, read, or hear. We never forget a name, a face, a person, or who they are, what they do, and where we met them. Our ability is a closely-guarded secret. You can't share your knowledge of our ability with anyone. Eight people have been killed by our bodyguards trying to kidnap Cliff and me. President Seaton knows of our ability, so we thought it's only right for you to know now that you're the vice president. I'm telling you because you may want our help from time to time," said Gloria.

"Holy crap, Gloria! Do you have anything else to knock me over with?"

"Yes. Hopefully, in the near future, we'll be able to provide you with a full-time assistant with the same ability, if you'd like one," said Gloria.

"Indeed, I would. Talk about a secret weapon!" smiled Aragon.

CHAPTER 23: FULL CIRCLE

A week after Sofia Aragon was sworn in as vice president, Cliff and Gloria's life fell into a routine. One of them was always at Gleason, while the other was either in Colorado or Kansas City.

Gloria frequently flew to her trucking empire to spend a week or two meeting with customers and learning about every aspect of the business. She expanded the company's customer base by being transparent about their cost and profit margin. She stressed the importance of protecting the customer's produce during loading and shipping. Gloria became directly involved with how the produce was packaged on the trucks so that it met the customer's approval. This personal touch went a long way in winning contracts with new or old customers. In her first year at the helm of the company, business grew 17% and profit was up 10%. The overall value of the company increased $26 million.

Marks was able to spend one week a month in Kansas City working on his four side jobs. Bonneville had clients for Cliff to interview, now that Robby had moved to Washington DC and was a full-time interrogator of foreign spies and operatives targeted by the CIA. Sometimes, his task was to stand next to a person the CIA was interested in and listen to the brain while at a social affair, in a crowded subway, or in an elevator. He came to Gleason often to be with Cliff, work out with him, enjoy the year-round access to the pool, and to graze on the delicious food. He knew that some female staffers liked to watch him in his Speedo. Robby's physique was even more toned than Stu's or Cliff's – and he loved to show it off. The Gleason staff adored him and went out of their way to please him. Every other month, he would fly back Kansas City to see Jameson, who constantly updated Robby's wardrobe. Robby was, without a doubt, the best-dressed man in the CIA, especially now that he had the money and the best advisor in Jameson.

Marks continued working with Dr. Westphal on comatose patient recovery. His batting average of success for getting patients to wake up was 65%. If the patient's brain was injured too badly, Marks's implants receivers could not hear anything due to little internal brain activity. He learned within a few minutes of listening to a comatose patient's brain if there was a chance of successfully waking them up. He came to accept the hard reality that he could help a patient with a severely damaged brain. Given time, some brains could heal themselves and become active. He waited two years for one patient's brain to heal enough, so that he could hear any internal activity; it was yet another year, though, before his implant could interact with that brain. He and Dr. Westphal were determined to save the 14-year-old boy who was injured in a fall from a treehouse.

The boy was 17 when Marks was finally able to wake him up.

Those rare events were gratifying, but hard on Marks's emotions. He slowly learned to be callous to the failures if he was going to continue this recovery work for years to come. As the emotional turmoil built up within him, Marks struggled with leaving his work at the hospital when he went home. To combat this, he met with his friend and psychiatrist, Dr. Molly Candle, who helped him learn to accept the failure when a patient was too far gone for his assistance.

Every month that Marks returned to his district, he solved a couple cold case crimes for the police department. It always baffled Captain Chesney how Marks quickly found the soft spot in people that the police suspected, but could never prove guilty. Chesney had learned to never ask how because he knew he would get double talk and a smile for an answer. In one murder case, the prime suspect's mind revealed where he had thrown the murder weapon in the river. It only took the department's body recovery drivers an hour to find the gun. Finding out that someone had lied to give a suspect an alibi was quite common and easy for Marks to uncover. Over a period of six years, he had made enough money from the comatose patient program and from solving crimes to repay the $5 million he had borrowed for his first political campaign, plus enough to afford living in Gleason, with a little help from Gloria's trucking company income.

Marks met with Tyka Packston, who Gloria had convinced to joined Syntil, to welcome her into the small, select group of successful implant recipients. He told her of his difficult introduction to the implant and the lessons learned the impact of the implant on his life and body. If she put her faith in Dr. Candle, her understanding of her capabilities and the implant's impact on her life would make things much smoother. After two months of rehabilitation from the car accident and numerous meetings with Dr. Candle, Tyka started working at the detective agency to practice her skills on clients. Marks knew she loved working with Gail and Bonneville.

While Tyka was getting used to her implant, she was also dealing with the loss of her right arm. She had several choices: an empty sleeve, an artificial limb, or undergo surgery to have a human arm grafted to her body – the functional capabilities of which would not be known until the arm was attached. Marks asked his surgical team at St. Luke's if they would graft a human arm on Tyka. She met with Dr. Westphal several times. He measured, recorded, explained the surgery, as well as the side effects of the medications she would have to take for her body to accept the new arm. After agreeing to the operation, it took several months before the right size, age, and complexion female arm became available. Dr. Westphal brought in two limb attachment experts. Dr. Westphal assisted in the exploratory operation of the stump of her arm to understand the condition and amount of useable vascular and nerve tissue in order to determine the attachment's chance of success.

Of course, the right arm for her right arm became available one dark, rainy night when a head-on collision killed three people. One was a female of Tyka's age and size. Dr. Westphal gathered the team together and the operation started at 1:00 a.m. the following morning.

It took three months for the arm to be at a useable state, although it was not as good as her left arm. Still, Tyka was happy with the outcome – and that was the most important objective. She thanked the doctors for giving her her arm back. She cried, raised her arm, and gripped their hands in gratitude.

All their efforts had one goal: to make Tyka's capabilities available full-time to the vice president and president.

After her arm healed from the surgery, Marks brought Tyka to Gleason to live for a month to get accustomed to the city. She spent time with Jerome and Becky Smoot to learn about the workings of Congress. Vice President Aragon had not asked for any help, so Marks did not take Tyka to meet her nor did he tell her that a full-time assistant was available.

President Seaton's health continued declining during his last year in office, so much that Vice President Aragon had to take the reins of running the government. His emphysema aggressively advanced to the point that he could not carry on a normal conversation. The 25th Amendment to the Constitution was invoked and Vice President Aragon became President Aragon.

Marks finally got a call from the new president for help.

Being the personal assistant to President Aragon was exciting and difficult for Tyka due to the number of people the president interacted with on a daily basis within the White House walls alone. She promptly discovered whose brain the president wanted her to monitor. The press, as well as the White House staff, were curious about who Tyka was and how she came to be a fixture around President Aragon. Tyka seldomly spoke, but was always writing notes she sometimes handed to her boss. The president typically stopped whatever she was doing to read Tyka's notes. No one else got to read the notes. President Aragon would read the note and then open the lower left drawer of the desk, where she had a shredder installed. Twice during a Cabinet meeting discussion, the president had turned to look behind her where Tyka sat and called her name. Tyka would come alive with a barrage of facts that either supported or countered what a Cabinet member was trying to promote. Only once did a Cabinet member take exception to Tyka's comments…and they lost badly in the exchange. The message was clear to the Cabinet members and the White House staff: You better have your facts straight or the president would turn her pitbull loose on you.

President Aragon soon realized that Tyka would be a perfect press secretary. Tyka knew what was going on in the administration and had total recall of every detail. There was not one member of the press who was smart enough to lead Tyka to misspeak, become confused, or make a mistake. Tyka knew exactly what she said yesterday and any other day at a press conference. A senior member of the press, who admired Tyka, asked how she had gone from homeless to special assistant to press secretary so quickly. "I am a disciple of Speaker Marks and now I serve the president."

"Are there other disciples?" the reported asked.

Tyka smiled and nodded her head.

From that day on, her nickname was 'The Disciple'. When she spoke, she spoke with the authority of President Aragon and House Speaker Marks.

Marks eventually grew weary of his position as Speaker of the House. When President Aragon's first term ended, she ran for re-election and asked Marks to join her on the ticket. He accepted.

He was ready for a new adventure.

www.ingramcontent.com/pod-product-compliance
Lightning Source LLC
Chambersburg PA
CBHW030247200626
46816CB00002BA/547